NO LEAVIN'
LOVE

By the Author

I Dare You

Visit us at www.boldstrokesbooks.com

What Reviewers Say About Bold Strokes Books

"With its expected unexpected twists, vivid characters and healthy dose of humor, *Blind Curves* is a very fun read that will keep you guessing." – *Bay Windows*

"In a succinct film style narrative, with scenes that move, a character-driven plot, and crisp dialogue worthy of a screenplay ... the Richfield and Rivers novels are ... an engaging Hollywood mystery ... series." – *Midwest Book Review*

Force of Nature "...is filled with nonstop, fast paced action. Tornadoes, raging fire blazes, heroic and daring rescues... Baldwin does a fine job of describing the fast-paced scenes and inspiring the reader to keep on turning the pages." – *L-word.comLiterature*

In the Jude Devine mystery series the "...characters seem fully capable of walking away from the particulars of whodunit and engaging the reader in other aspects of their lives." – *Lambda Book Report*

Mine "...weaves a tale of yearning, love, lust, and conflict resolution ... a believable plot, with strong characters in a charming setting." – *JustAboutWrite*

"While these two women struggle with their issues, there is some very, very hot sex. If you enjoy complex characters and passionate sex scenes, you'll love *Wild Abandon*." – *MegaScene*

"*Course of Action* is a romance ... populated with a host of captivating and amiable characters. The glimpses into the lifestyles of the rich and beautiful people are rather like guilty pleasures ... a most satisfying and entertaining reading experience." – *Midwest Book Review*

The Clinic is "...a spellbinding novel." – *JustAboutWrite*

"*Unexpected Sparks* lived up to its promise and was thoroughly enjoyable ... Dartt did a lovely job at building the relationship between Kate and Nikki." – *Lambda Book Report*

"*Sequestered Hearts* ... is everything a romance should be. It is teeming with longing, heartbreak, and of course, love. As pure romances go, it is one of the best in print today." – *L-word.comLiterature*

"*The Exile and the Sorcerer* is a mesmerizing read, a tour-de-force packed with adventure, ordeals, complex twists and turns, and the internal introspection of appealing characters." – *Midwest Book Review*

The Spanish Pearl is "...both science fiction and romance in this adventurous tale ... A most entertaining read, with a sequel already in the works. Hot, hot, hot!" – *Minnesota Literature*

"A deliciously sexy thriller ... *Dark Valentine* is funny, scary, and very realistic. The story is tightly written and keeps the reader gripped to the exciting end." – *JustAbout Write*

"*Punk Like Me* ... is different. It is engaging. It is life-affirming. Frankly, it is genius. This is a rare book in that it has a soul; one that is laid bare for all to see." – *JustAboutWrite*

"*Chance* is not a novel about the music industry; it is about a woman discovering herself as she muddles through all the trappings of fame." – *Midwest Book Review*

Sweet Creek "... is sublimely in tune with the times." – *Q-Syndicate*

"*Forever Found* ... neatly combines hot sex scenes, humor, engaging characters, and an exciting story." – *MegaScene*

Shield of Justice is a "...well-plotted...lovely romance...I couldn't turn the pages fast enough!" – Ann Bannon, author of *The Beebo Brinker Chronicles*

The 100th Generation is "...filled with ancient myths, Egyptian gods and goddesses, legends, and, most wonderfully, it contains the lesbian equivalent of Indiana Jones living and working in modern Egypt." – *Just About Write*

Sword of the Guardian is "...a terrific adventure, coming of age story, a romance, and tale of courtly intrigue, attempted assassination, and gender confusion ... a rollicking fun book and a must-read for those who enjoy courtly light fantasy in a medieval-seeming time." – *Midwest Book Review*

"*Of Drag Kings and the Wheel of Fate*'s lush rush of a romance incorporates reincarnation, a grounded transman and his peppy daughter, and the dark moods of a troubled witch—wonderful homage to Leslie Feinberg's classic gender-bending novel, *Stone Butch Blues*." – *Q-Syndicate*

In *Running with the Wind* "...the discussions of the nature of sex, love, power, and sexuality are insightful and represent a welcome voice from the view of late-20-something characters today." – *Midwest Book Review*

"Rich in character portrayal, *The Devil Inside* is an unusual, unpredictable, and thought-provoking love story that will have the reader questioning the definition of right and wrong long after she finishes the book." – *JustAboutWrite*

Wall of Silence "...is perfectly plotted and has a very real voice and consistently accurate tone, which is not always the case with lesbian mysteries." – *Midwest Book Review*

NO LEAVIN'
LOVE

by

Larkin Rose

2009

NO LEAVIN' LOVE
© 2009 BY LARKIN ROSE. ALL RIGHTS RESERVED.

ISBN 10: 1-60282-079-1
ISBN 13: 978-1-60282-079-1

THIS TRADE PAPERBACK ORIGINAL IS PUBLISHED BY
BOLD STROKES BOOKS, INC.
P.O. BOX 249
VALLEY FALLS, NY 12185

FIRST EDITION: MAY 2009

CREDITS
EDITORS: JENNIFER KNIGHT AND STACIA SEAMAN
PRODUCTION DESIGN: STACIA SEAMAN
COVER DESIGN BY SHERI (GRAPHICARTIST2020@HOTMAIL.COM)

Acknowledgments

A big thank you to the editors—you take the rough and smooth it to a gleaming masterpiece. You always rock!

Dedication

To Radclyffe: thank you for seeing that "something" in my writing and giving it the chance to breathe beyond my computer screen…again. You're amazing and I treasure my role in your family.

To the BSB readers, and especially "my" readers: once again, everything I've written, I've written Just…For…You!

To my family: without you, my heart would be empty. I love each and every one of you more than you could ever possibly know.

To Tammy: thanks for your "horsey" help.

To Jove Belle: for being an awesome brainstorming, plotting, and outlining buddy—thank you soooo much!

To India Masters: for your hilarious sarcasm that I can never get enough of. Love ya, mean it!

To Dalia Craig: for your endless late-night help and priceless friendship. Muah!

And always, to Rose. Your love and support is all I ever need. I love you.

Chapter One

Mercedes shoved the silky-skinned brunette until the back of her knees met the edge of the bed and she went sprawling across the mattress. *Shit.* What was her name? Jennifer...Jessica? Not that it mattered. After tonight, they'd never see each other again anyway. Too much work...too little time. A good, satisfying fuck was all she was interested in. Mercedes climbed over the woman and straddled her athletic thighs. She needed to come, and hard, and dear God, soon. The past week had been a bitch. Two crime scenes. A wasted day in court. And tomorrow she was supposed to present a PowerPoint session on the interpretation and recording of impact blood spatter for a group of trainee crime scene technicians.

These days she was no longer sure why she'd chosen a career in forensics. Her work had fascinated her in the beginning but now, after five years of specialization in her field, she was feeling jaded.

Mercedes looked down into the sultry fuck-me eyes of the woman beneath her and realized it had been weeks since she'd brought a woman home, maybe even months. Hell if she could remember. Seemed like the weeks merged into one another lately.

Jennifer, or Jessica, grinned up at her. "Damn, baby. I see

you like your sex a little rough." She grabbed Mercedes's hips and flipped her onto her back, then straddled her.

"I just like it fast, direct, and to the point." Mercedes tugged at the woman's shirt until she shrugged out of it.

A name tag fell from the pocket. "Jessica" had an all-events pass to some convention she was in town for. She removed her sports bra, freeing breasts that would fit perfectly in Mercedes's cupped hands, even more deliciously in her mouth. Dark nipples hardened under her gaze. Mercedes licked her lips and eased forward. She curled her tongue around one disc, then sucked the pebbled creation into her mouth. Jessica moaned and arched, grinding her hips down against Mercedes.

Mercedes released her hold. "I need you to fuck me."

With a wicked smile, Jessica kneed Mercedes's legs apart and pumped against her, tugging her hips in a firm grip with each hard thrust. "With pleasure."

"Oh, God, yes. Make me come!" Mercedes met her thrusts, desperate for release, out of her mind with need.

"No worries, sexy. I'm going to make you scream." Jessica tugged the clasp of Mercedes's slacks and eased them down her legs. "And the next time I'm in town, let's hook up. I'd be more than happy to scratch this itch anytime." She winked as if she knew that scenario would never occur.

Damn. Was Mercedes that transparent, sending out the "one-time only" message? She shrugged off the question. Of course, and the message left no doubt in anybody's mind that there was no place in her life for anything other than a quick fuck to ease her frustration, then good-bye.

Mercedes could feel how wet her pussy was. She wanted fingers buried inside her, making her come…making her scream with release. She kicked her pants off her feet and locked her legs around the brunette's waist, thrusting her pussy against hard abs. Dear God, she was so close to exploding. Jessica shimmied down her body, forcing Mercedes's legs further apart. Almost there…almost riding the waves of seduction.

When the phone shrilled from beside the bed, Mercedes growled. *Not now!* She needed this free time, needed this wild "never going to see you again" sex. Interruptions wouldn't do tonight. She ignored the harsh rings and focused on the woman lying between her thighs. The woman slid her fingers along the edge of her thong, pulled it to the side, and teased her wet pussy with a single digit. When her hot mouth clamped down over her clit, Mercedes sucked in her breath and fisted her hands.

The phone continued its loud demand.

"Do you need to get that?"

"Hell no, they can wait." Mercedes circled her hips to emphasize her need.

Two long fingers shoved their slippery way inside.

Mercedes let loose a sharp cry and arched against the mattress. "Yes! Fuck me, please!"

When the phone stopped ringing, she entwined her fingers in the woman's short, disheveled hair and pumped her hips faster. Her orgasm built, teetering on the edge.

The phone started ringing again.

With a heavy moan, Mercedes slapped her hands against the mattress. "Fuck!" She slipped out from under the woman and yanked up the receiver. "What do you want?"

"Is that any way to greet your daddy?"

Mercedes sat straight up on the bed, suddenly aware of every naked inch of her skin. What was it about her father's voice that always made her feel like she was being busted sneaking through a window in the middle of night?

"Sorry, Daddy. I've, um, been getting prank callers lately."

She gave Jessica an "I need to take this" shrug and rolled away from her. "How are you?"

"I'm great, and you? We haven't heard from you in weeks."

Mercedes's heart cramped into a knot. Guilt plagued her as she got to her feet and moved toward the bedroom door. "Sorry. Work's crazy lately."

"Work should never come between you and family. Don't you think it's time to come home for a visit? It's only been, what, thirteen years?"

Mercedes looked toward the ceiling. Thirteen years still wasn't long enough. There wasn't a damn thing on that ranch she missed except him, and of course, her sister, Darlene. But even they couldn't make her return. Their every-other-year family vacations to anywhere but Colorado were plenty fulfilling. Mercedes didn't need to smell cow manure to feel like she was connecting with her family.

"That's not fair, Daddy," she said. "You know how busy I am. Besides, we'll be seeing each other in Florida at the end of this year."

Her father chuckled. "Well, seems your little surprise vacations are the only way I'm going to see my baby. What choice do I have? No telling what you spend for them fancy hotels and tours. Though I must admit playing golf in Phoenix last time was fun."

Mercedes smiled. Her father was a prideful man, couldn't stand his children paying for anything. "Those trips are worth every dime. Besides, what's a little money compared to spending time with my daddy?"

"I'm getting married."

Her father's words ricocheted around her head like a pinball whizzing from pin to pin. A lump lodged in her throat. "You're what? You can't get married!"

"Who says? I'm a ripe ol' age."

"What about…" Mercedes clamped her mouth shut. Mentioning her mother wasn't fair. Her death had been hard on all of them, hardest on her dad.

God, how Mercedes missed her. Her mom was the real reason Mercedes had worked her ass off to climb the ladder of success. Elizabeth Miller had wanted her baby to be something more than just a rancher's daughter, wanted her independent and strong-willed. Mercedes had achieved her wishes.

"Honey, it's past time for me to go on with my life," her father said. "Nelda has made me a happy man again."

"Nelda? Who the hell is Nelda?" Mercedes trapped a groan in her throat and paced, the hard-on for the woman still waiting on her bed gone. There wouldn't be any more sex in her itinerary tonight. She found her clothes and got dressed. Her date took the hint and began to do the same.

"Nelda Roberts is the woman I'm marrying. We've been seeing each other for a while now."

"Oh my God, you date?" The thought left a sour taste in her mouth. There wasn't a woman alive who could take the place of her mother, God rest her loving soul.

"Yes, sweetie, I date. I go to the movies, out to dinner, curl up on the couch to watch late-night flicks. Even share breakfast in the morning."

Mercedes scoffed. "Daddy! You can't possibly be serious."

"Serious as a heart attack, and we'd like you to join us for our wedding. In two weekends, to be exact."

"Two weeks? You've got to be fucking kidding!"

Jessica finished buttoning her shirt, picked up her purse, and stepped past her. "I'll let myself out."

Seconds later the front door closed with firm finality. *Damn it! There goes my fuck.*

"Why in the hell haven't you bothered to mention any of this before now?" Mercedes demanded.

"Watch that mouth of yours, girlie." His stern voice was like ice daggers even over a fiber optic cable. "And I did try. If you'd answer your phone once in a blue moon, you'd know that. I also sent you an invitation, but I'm assuming you were too busy to read it?"

Mercedes cut her gaze toward the stand by the front door, the catchall for mail not pressing enough to read immediately. Normally she opened her daddy's letters the day they arrived. She stalked over, remembering an oversized parchment envelope she'd tossed aside a while ago. She'd thought it was a promotional offer from one of the tour companies she'd contacted while she was planning the Florida vacation.

"Sorry." Mercedes located the envelope and inspected it. Her father's scrawling handwriting was missing. Instead, someone had stuck a tiny printed address label in the top corner.

"I'd really like you to meet Nelda. She's one helluva woman."

"Uh-huh." Mercedes stomped into the kitchen and yanked a Mountain Dew from the refrigerator. She popped the top and took a long, cooling swallow.

"I know you'll get along great with her." A long pause followed. Mercedes could envision him scratching his chin in concentration. "Can I expect you? It would mean a lot to have my baby girl here for my wedding."

"Daddy, I can't just drop everything. I'm due in court on a big case soon."

"The carnival's in town. You wouldn't want to miss that."

Mercedes rolled her eyes. She didn't have freaking time

to be line dancing, or watching little brats rush about to win the next stuffed animal. Worse, she couldn't stand the thought of going back to that damn stinky ranch…or seeing the woman who was now her daddy's foreman, the main reason she avoided going home.

Sydney Campbell.

Even the sound of her name sent quivers through her body. First of lust, then of total aggravation. She was the one girl Mercedes could never best all those years ago no matter how hard she tried. Sydney was out and damn proud when Mercedes was still trying to feel her way with her sexuality. Sure, she'd been curious, but not enough to test the waters for a long while, though she couldn't deny her nightly thoughts took her there…with Sydney.

The summer before the plane took her away to college, everything had changed. Syd had found her reading under an oak tree, and there, in the shade, she'd proven Mercedes was a closet case waiting to be unleashed. For many nights after that, they'd met in the same spot and explored each other further. Jesus, she'd never forget how hard she used to come, and how lonely she'd been when Syd never called her.

She wished she'd never left that note stabbed to "their" tree with the very hairpin Syd had torn loose from her head, claiming she needed to feel every strand sifting across her face while Mercedes came. The words she'd written echoed in her mind.

Thank you for making me forget how miserable I am in this shithole town. You could really make me believe this is the place I belong, but I would end up resenting that, and you, and I can't risk that. The future I want is already mapped out and you know it.

By the time you get this note, I will be starting that new beginning.

I'm sorry, but I can't say good-bye to you. As hard as this is to admit to myself, let alone to you, I can't stop thinking about you...or our nights.

Please call me. Would love to hear your voice. And your late-night moans.

Mercedes

Mercedes scrunched her nose and sniffed. How pathetic a note could she have left? She'd all but begged the bitch to call her...to chase her. What the hell had she been thinking when she wrote that stupid shit? What a loser she sounded like.

Fuck Sydney Campbell. *She'd* moved on and made a fantastic life for herself and Syd was still stuck in that one horse town. Mercedes hesitated. She knew she'd been running from her past for too long. Maybe it was time to show Sydney what she was missing out on. She could eat her fucking heart out.

Furthermore, whoever this Nelda was, she was making a mistake if she thought she could sweet-talk her way into marriage and a ranch. After Mercedes was done with her, Nelda would tuck her tail between her legs and forget Travis Miller existed.

With a smile on her face and her mind expanding with the many malicious ways she could make this wannabe stepmom go away, Mercedes said, "I love you, Daddy, and I wouldn't miss it for the world." Her voice dripped with sarcasm but he didn't seem to notice.

"How soon can you get here, sweetheart?"

Mercedes gripped the receiver tighter in her grasp. "As soon as my boss lets me go."

She dropped the phone in its cradle and gulped down the rest of her Mountain Dew. The knot in her stomach tightened as she slinked into the chair at the dining table. What in the hell had she just agreed to?

Chapter Two

Mercedes held the cell phone away from her ear while her sister, Darlene, shouted, "I'm not kidding, missy. Your ass better be on that plane."

"I'm at the frickin' airport, aren't I?"

Mercedes stepped back while an elderly gentleman escorted a woman across the pedestrian walkway in front of the airport. His hand rested in the small of her back while she shuffled along at a snail's pace. Memories flooded her mind. She could still see her father stealing romantic kisses from her mother when he thought no one was looking—a small swat to her ass, their happy smiles. She swallowed the lump rising in her throat. If only her mom could have lived long enough to watch Mercedes walk across that stage to accept her diploma, or appear in court as a professional respected in her field.

Her mother had known Mercedes's fate as soon as she was born, and had given her a name that would fit her for life. Mercedes, a cowgirl in a fancy car; that's what her Elizabeth Miller knew she'd be one day. She'd so desperately wanted Mercedes to succeed that she'd made all kinds of sacrifices. Both her parents had. Mercedes wished she'd shown them more gratitude instead of giving her father shit about helping on the ranch, practically refusing to assist in any ranch chore, which only caused her mother to jump to her defense when her daddy put his foot down and gave that cold, dark stare he'd mastered…probably immediately after Mercedes's birth.

She truly couldn't have loved either one of them more, yet looking back, Mercedes thought she'd probably given them both nothing but grief, acting like a spoiled brat instead of the tough, self-reliant girl her father had raised her to be. Hell, she wasn't sure now which of her parents had given her those qualities. They were both headstrong and stubborn, and always fought for what they wanted.

Tears sprang to her eyes as she reminisced. She'd left the ranch thirteen years ago determined to attain everything her mother had dreamed of. Her country drawl had turned a few heads when she first walked into the LAPD. Even now, eight years later, people still asked if she was from the South, as though nothing but country hicks were spawned from "down there." But she had the perfect condo and nothing but the finest designer labels in her closet. She lived life in a courtroom, a crime scene, or in the lab, with a full caseload occupying her analytical mind, and quick fucks on the side when her sexual cravings needed satisfying. She should be happy and content, but she hadn't felt that way since she'd boarded that plane for college and left behind the only life she'd ever known, and a mother who had only wanted the very best for her daughter.

If Mercedes could give it all up, every stitch of clothing, every penny of her fat bank account, to have just one more day with her mom, she would in the blink of an eye. She'd done everything…she still did everything for the one person who would never see her accomplishments.

Plane engines whined in the distance, yanking her from a past she couldn't change. Mercedes realized she hadn't heard anything her sister said for a few minutes, not that Darlene was waiting on her opinions. She hadn't stopped for breath between telling Mercedes how to live her life and guilt-tripping her about not visiting the ranch. With her teeth gritted, Mercedes tuned in. Darlene had nothing new to say, so she'd switched to one of her favorite rants.

"Daddy worked his tail off to send you to that highfalutin' college that led you to your highfalutin' job so you could afford your highfalutin' perfect condo."

"You could have gone away to college, too," Mercedes said.

Darlene was the apple of their father's eye, and the spitting image of their beautiful mother with her free-flying dark copper curls, sherry brown eyes, and dots of freckles on her chiseled nose. She was the perfect child who jumped every time their daddy pointed. Her grades had sucked to hell and back, mainly because all she thought about was the ranch, the chores she had to do on the ranch, what horse was due to birth, which horses were ready to train. Jesus, but the girl had lived and breathed that fucking ranch to the point that she finally left high school early to be a full-time ranch hand. Well, that wasn't Mercedes's fault.

Resentfully, Darlene muttered, "Well, not all of us get a career handed to us on a silver platter. Some of us actually have to sweat for a living."

"And some of us choose to sweat unnecessarily."

"But we're not talking about hardworking people, now are we, Mercedes?" Darlene snapped back. "The least you can do is show up for Daddy's ding-dang wedding!"

"Daddy isn't marrying anybody," Mercedes said slowly. "Ms. Nelda is going back to wherever the hell she came from. I'll make sure of it."

"You better leave them alone," Darlene warned. "And so help me, if I have to fly to that smog-filled city myself, I'll stomp your ass all the way back home and hogtie you to the chair while Daddy says 'I do.'"

"Tell me something, Darlene," Mercedes said sarcastically. "Did it ever cross your little mind that Daddy's been lonely and this woman's just dug her claws in? I guarantee she doesn't love him."

"This coming from the country-turned-city girl who left us all behind. Like you're ever here to even know what the hell you're talking about," Darlene said smugly. "Now, are you going to get your high-society ass on that flight or do I get to put these boots to use?"

"I'm getting on the fucking plane, so stop your damn yapping."

"Watch that filthy mouth. Hasn't it got you in enough trouble your whole life?"

Darlene loved reminding Mercedes that she was the problem child who always got in trouble. They'd been oil and water since Darlene was old enough to refuse to wear anything resembling girlie, and Mercedes had refused to wear Rustlers or Levi's, or anything made of denim, and then demanded everyone take off their shoes at the front door as to not scuff the hardwood floors.

Darlene wore nothing but Wranglers, had picnics in the hills behind their farmhouse, and skinny-dipped in the stream out back of old man Potter's ranch. Her heart was rooted to home. But Mercedes detested cowboy boots, home on the range, or anything to do with horses and cattle, and had steered clear of her father at all costs for fear that he might make her do the unthinkable, like cleaning the stables. How she was born a rancher's daughter she'd never understand.

Mercedes stared at the automatic sliding doors. Beyond them, a silver bird, destined for the sky, was waiting to carry her back to the smelly, dirty wild west. Great.

"I'm turning my cell phone off," she told Darlene and

snapped the phone shut, choking off the sound of her sister's loud response.

With a deep sigh, she entered the airport. After getting her seat assignment and checking her luggage, she joined the line to pass through security. Her thoughts wandered as she absently followed the people in front of her, removing her shoes and waiting to be waved through the metal detector. What would Sydney Campbell look like now? Was she still as sexy as she was all those years ago with her lean swagger and strong tanned arms? God, how she'd worked those hands. Mercedes shivered as she recalled Syd's fingers buried inside her.

With heat flushing her cheeks, she reminded herself that Syd had never called. She'd made her point, and Mercedes had gone on with her life...just as planned. Despite her anxiety about going home, and seeing Syd again, Mercedes smiled. Syd was the least of her worries. She had more fish to fry with her trip back to that damn ranch.

Poor Nelda Roberts wasn't going to know what hit her.

❖

Sydney turned her horse toward the stables. God, how she loved the outdoors and this ranch—any ranch, for that matter. But especially this one. She couldn't imagine working for a better man than Travis Miller. An honest, hardworking employer, he treated all of his employees with utmost respect. Moreover, being foreman kept her busy enough that she didn't think too often about the ranch in Larimer County that should have been hers, the one she grew up on. Her father hadn't trusted a woman to do a man's job, no matter how many years of her life she'd done just that, working for him. Instead, upon his death, he'd left her his life insurance and handed the ranch she loved over to her drunk of a brother, who'd bankrupted them within five years. Sydney had been left with nothing except his old, beat-up Ford pickup.

For several years after his death, she'd lived off the insurance money and self-pity. Her heartbreak was for the loss of her dreams rather than a father who drank and smoked himself into an early grave. Unfeeling, maybe, but true. He'd made those choices. Worse, he'd never believed in her abilities and had left her to live with the consequences.

Once she finally cowboyed up to the cold, hard facts, she went in search of work and Travis Miller hadn't hesitated hiring her. She worked hard, and steady, and made foreman in the blink of an eye. Miller believed in her, and she'd never let him down. He knew her dream was to one day own something as fine as his ranch, and that somehow, someday, she would achieve that goal.

In the meantime, she was content with the twenty acres Miller had sold her, and the cabin she'd built with her own sweat and blood. He would have given her the land but she was too prideful to take charity and saved every dime for five years to pay him a fair price. Tucked into the farthest corner of the ranch, she was close enough to assist with any emergency yet far enough away to feel independent. The distance also assured her of privacy, so no one would hear the penetrating sounds of her one-night stands.

Syd shook off the thoughts that weighed her down. The past was the past and she'd be damned if she'd look back when the future was waiting for her. She glanced around at the graceful two-story Miller homestead, which loomed against the vast Colorado sky. Designed by Miller's late wife, Elizabeth, to blend with the land rather than shout, "Look at me," the house was set on a gentle slope with views across more than three hundred acres of grassy slopes and beautiful wilderness to the Front Ranges and the soaring snow-capped Rocky Mountains beyond. Miller had put a pool and hot tub in the backyard surrounded by an eight-foot privacy fence, and Elizabeth, his late wife, had planted a spectacular alpine garden out front. She was a wonderful woman with a heart of gold, and Syd was proud to have called her a friend. She still missed her.

Now Miller was marrying again to a sweetheart of a woman, and through their morning meetings, he'd hinted about being ready to retire. Syd knew she shouldn't get her hopes up about a possible role in the management of the ranch. Miller had two daughters, one of whom was perfectly capable of running an operation as big as the D&M Cattle Company. Darlene would take over, Syd was sure of that. But Darlene would need help and that other bitch of a daughter, Mercedes, had never shown any interest in ranching.

Syd huffed. As far as she was concerned, Mercedes Miller wasn't fit to wipe her daddy's boots. At this very moment, the little bitch was somewhere in the sky, on the way back home for her daddy's wedding, probably resentful as hell that she had to make the trip. She never visited the ranch and Sydney didn't know why she was bothering to turn up for the wedding. What did she care about Miller's happiness? There was only one person Mercedes cared about, and that was Mercedes.

Sydney ground her teeth in irritation as her mind whiplashed to the past and her pussy clenched in remembrance. She hadn't seen Mercedes since their animalistic fucks beneath the oak tree over thirteen years ago. God, the sounds Mercedes had made would forever burn a hole through her. Sex had taken on a new meaning with every moan of pleasure beneath the watchful eye of the moon and the cool mountain breezes. Their exploration of one another seemed endless, pure, and satisfying. Then one day, Mercedes was gone... off to college to earn a degree toward her high-paying career. She'd never even said good-bye.

For some odd reason, Sydney thought their nights together might have meant something to the self-centered bitch. Boy, had she been wrong. That chickenshit coward didn't even care enough to have a conversation about what was happening between them. She'd just bolted like a quarter horse hurtling off the starting line. Sydney knew she shouldn't still hold a grudge after all these years, and she knew she was probably nothing more than a summer experiment for Miller's daughter, someone beneath her and easily discarded. But just thinking about being face-to-face with Mercedes didn't sit easy in the pit of her stomach. She'd felt something on those nights, felt Mercedes's guard crumble while she clung to her like a life preserver. Those moans of satisfaction had plagued Sydney for years, even when she brought other women to her bed, trying to erase the memories.

Oh well, best to leave the past in the past. Syd had moved on and was content with her life just the way it was. She had work she loved and a few pacifying fucks here and there. Life couldn't get better than that. No hassles, no problems.

The sound of pebbles crunching beneath tires pulled her away from her thoughts and she looked over her shoulder to see a sleek black car speeding down Miller's long driveway, plumes of dust spiraling in its wake. When the car slid to a halt in front of the house, Sydney turned her horse around to get a better view of the woman she hadn't seen in years. The driver's door opened and a black high-heeled pump appeared beneath the edge. Mercedes stood, cell phone pressed against her ear. Could she look any more edible? Her gorgeous sandy brown hair was twisted into a tight librarian's bun, but Sydney knew what those strands looked like cascading down her bare back, over those olive shoulders, and disheveled around her face after a hard fuck. Jesus. This was going to be the longest week of her life.

She took a deep breath and held her head high. Mercedes might look totally fuckable, but she'd be damned if she fell into that trap again. Beauty was only skin deep, and Mercedes had a tongue more poisonous than a snakebite. Sydney tapped her heel to the mare's flank and trotted with ease toward the woman ranting into her cell.

"I most certainly will not call your superior or anyone else in your office!" Mercedes yelled. "You will send a decent mechanic to 129 Rocking Chair Lane to fix this fucking air conditioner by the end of the day or you will be hearing from my lawyer. I rented an operable vehicle, not one that sputtered hot air all over me."

Mercedes yanked open the back door and dropped several large bags to the ground. She stopped and slammed her manicured hand on her hip, still complaining. "Let me explain this once again. Unless you like standing in the unemployment line, I suggest you get your ass on the phone to a mechanic and get this rental fixed ASAP. Am I making myself clear, Cindy, or whatever the hell your name is?"

Without another word, she snapped the cell phone shut and let out an exasperated sigh. Syd smiled. Mercedes hadn't changed a bit—still had that fiery, sarcastic wit. Syd knew how to tame that tiger…knew what she sounded like when she was coming and out of control.

Mercedes jerked up a bag. "Fucking people."

She slung the bag over her shoulder and reached for the other. But the weight of the duffel knocked her off balance and she flailed her arms in the air in an attempt to break her fall. Too late. The bag pulled her backward and before Sydney could offer assistance, Mercedes was flat on her ass in the gravel.

"Goddamn it!" she cursed.

Sydney moved the horse closer. God, she wanted to fuck the fire right out of Mercedes…just like she had so many years ago.

❖

Mercedes raised a hand to shield her eyes from the setting sun and stared up at the silhouette of someone on a horse standing over her. A woman, for sure. Those tanned arms were too small to be a man's…but a woman in damn good shape if the muscles coursing down them told her anything at all.

The rider dismounted with a smooth grace and landed on the ground. She walked closer, her Stetson briefly blocking the sun, and then extended her hand in invitation as her face came into view.

Mercedes bit back a gasp as her gaze settled on Sydney Campbell. Hot damn, but the woman sure had filled out. She was built like a fucking brick shithouse. Mercedes all but forgot her name and how to breathe as she took the casually offered hand and allowed Syd to pull her from the ground.

"Welcome back, Mercedes."

Mercedes only stared in shock, too overwhelmed with memories to utter a word. Her mind was overflowing dangerously fast with images of Syd's lips parted in pleasure… how her brow creased right before she came.

Oh, yeah, coming back here was a mistake.

"You okay?" Syd still held her hand.

Mercedes came back to herself with a rush and pulled her fingers from Syd's calloused grip. "Yep. Just fine. You can get back to whatever chore you were doing." She brushed off her ass and legs, her pussy pulsing with need.

Syd chuckled. "Will do. And thanks for the show. Watching an uppity city girl flop around in the pebbles like a pig in slop was very entertaining." She mounted her horse and adjusted herself in the saddle. "By the way, sweetheart, you got a run in your expensive stockings."

Mercedes jerked around to glare at her. "I'm sure my discomfiture was the highlight of your day, seeing as how you have nothing better to do with your time but mooch off my daddy."

Syd winked and tipped her hat, displaying the beginning signs of sexy salt-and-pepper hair. "Yep. That's all I'm good for at this here ranch."

She clicked her tongue and turned her horse. With firm legs clamped around the horse's sides, away she went.

Watching her canter off toward the sunset, Mercedes ignored her mind screaming to call her back, her heart demanding she forget the whole incident happened. That woman didn't deserve an ounce of her irritation. She hadn't even tried to get in touch after Mercedes left for college. Not that Mercedes had wanted her to, but somehow it still hurt, or maybe her ego was damaged. She stared down at her bags. Getting away from this place was the best thing she'd ever done, and Syd could have done the same thing…*if* she'd wanted her.

"Mercedes!" Her daddy raced down the porch steps and ran toward her.

Her heart cramped to see how youthful he still was. Tears sprang to her eyes as she took a careful step on the pebbles toward him. He crushed her in his arms and flung her around as if she was a kid again. God, he had a way of making her feel so much younger than her thirty-three years.

He set her back on her feet and held her out for an examination. "You okay? I saw that nasty fall you took."

"I'm fine, Daddy. I'm a tough girl, you know that." She chucked his chin and reached for a bag.

He stepped around her and grabbed the remaining luggage. "Too tough, sometimes. I worry about you."

She looked over her shoulder at the man she adored. He was the best man she knew. There was no one above him in her eyes. "I'm doing great, Daddy. Put your concerns toward more important things."

The screen door creaked and a quaint little woman stepped out onto the porch. She had sky blue eyes and a smile to mend broken hearts. Her short brown hair was neatly combed down on the sides of her face with a shading of bangs across her forehead. Mercedes was immediately impressed with the bold gray highlights she saw shimmering against the sun. Only a self-confident woman could pull off wearing her natural hair color in such a fashion. Overwhelming happiness was sheltered in the woman's expression. Mercedes was taken back by the gentle, unforced smile. She looked so sweet, and so thrilled to be meeting her.

"Nelda, this is my baby girl, Mercedes."

Mercedes plastered a fake smile on her face and climbed the four steps to the porch, her daddy close by her side.

Poor, poor Nelda. That sweet little face wouldn't halt the bitch ready to unleash from within Mercedes. There wasn't a woman alive she'd allow to take her mother's place, not even a sweetheart the likes of Ms. Nelda.

There would be no wedding. Nelda was going back home…and very soon.

CHAPTER THREE

Mercedes dropped her bag and stared at Nelda, who stood with her arms open in invitation, that sweet smile dominating her rounded face. *Jesus*, did she really have to hug the woman she was about to run off the ranch, hopefully within the hour? She caught her daddy's cocked brow and let out a sigh. Unable to bear his disappointment, she ground her teeth and stepped into Nelda's open arms.

"Oh, honey." Nelda squeezed her, rubbed her back, then held her at arm's length. "Your daddy has gone on and on about you. He says you have a tongue quicker than a strike of lightning." She winked and hugged Mercedes again, whispering softly, "Give it your best shot, darlin'."

Mercedes recognized the challenge in her words as she pulled out of the embrace and hurried into the house. That underlying tone warned her to back off. Too bad this woman didn't know her like the rest of her family. Let the games begin.

A door banged loudly from the second floor, followed by a staccato of bare feet against the stairs, and then Darlene bolted around the corner into the foyer. "Oh, my God! You're here!" She flung her arms around Mercedes neck and bounced like a teenager.

Another pang of guilt choked Mercedes as she laughed and returned the hug. She'd once been so close to Darlene, sharing secrets only sisters could share. Darlene was the only person who knew about her romps in the woods with Sydney and what a fool she'd been to await Syd's phone call.

Shirking the thoughts, she released Darlene and gave her the once-over. Tears threatened while she stared into the mirror image of her mother. Darlene's copper hair was still cut in a short bob, trimmed neatly around her narrow face. Though her freckles had multiplied from the sun, her underlying tan was still rich and deep. My God, how time flew by yet stood breathlessly still while everything else seemed to keep moving. Mercedes fended off the uncomfortable thought that she should be ashamed of herself for abandoning Darlene and her father as she'd done.

Darlene's nostrils flared as her gaze swept Mercedes from head to toe then back again. "You ain't wearing those la-di-da clothes all weekend. We're going shopping tomorrow for some skintight jeans and proper boots." She touched the collar of Mercedes's shirt and pursed her lips. "My sister ain't showing up at the street dance wearing this crap."

Mercedes rolled her eyes. "I'll forgo on what passes for amusement out here in the sticks, thank you. Besides, I'm here to visit Daddy, not attend a hick county fair."

Her father came indoors and put the remaining bags down. "If you plan on visiting with me, you'll be going to the carnival. That's where we'll all be. No matter how quaint you find our entertainment, darlin', you'll be respectful of the folks you've known all your life." He stepped around Mercedes and pulled Nelda against his side, smiling lovingly at the woman Mercedes wanted to toss into the cow manure. "Nelda will be entering the baking contest and then we're going to do a little two-stepping."

His eyes gleamed with happiness. Mercedes hadn't seen that spark in a long time, nor had she heard it so obvious in his voice. Maybe she should rethink her plans. But when her gaze caught Nelda's, the one that said *I ain't going anywhere, you spoiled little brat*, Mercedes promised herself she would meet that challenge, and then some.

"Come on, Nelda made cookies." Darlene grabbed Mercedes's arm and pulled her toward the kitchen.

Mouthwatering aromas met her as they pushed through the swinging door. Mercedes hadn't smelled anything so delicious in years—probably since her mother was alive. She glanced past the island range and around the cabinets lining the wall, feeling the absence of her mother. The glass angel figurines Elizabeth Miller had always kept on the windowsill to catch the afternoon rays were gone. The walls were bare of the elementary school paintings she'd insisted on having framed to preserve their messy beauty. She'd always said Mercedes and Darlene had artistic talent. God love her, she was so biased about her children she'd never admit a two-year-old could have painted a better picture.

The banishment of her mother's keepsakes sent anger bubbling through Mercedes like hot lava. How dare this usurper come into their home and take away things that her mother, as well as her father, treasured? She cut a glare toward Nelda, who seemed occupied with checking something in the double oven. "Where are my mother's treasures?"

"Oh, I moved those things to a better location, dear." She finished inspecting whatever was making saliva rush to Mercedes's mouth, then rose, that sickening sweet smile plastered on her face.

Darlene shoved a cookie under Mercedes's nose. "Here, taste this."

Mercedes accepted the offering ungraciously and caught

Darlene's "don't do it" narrowed eyes. She took a small bite, letting the flavor savor on her tongue for several mouth-watering seconds before she turned back to Nelda. "Mmm. Delicious. Very dense, but tasty. I'd forgotten how heavy country cooking can be." She tossed the remaining portion of the cookie in the trash and turned to her father. "Which reminds me, Daddy, how's your cholesterol these days? Mom always took care to make sure you ate healthy."

His expression told her she was treading on thin ice. She gave him her best angelic smile. With an impatient sigh, he said, "I'll have you know my cholesterol is fine thanks to Nelda's no-fat cooking."

Nelda giggled. The sound resembled something from a school playground at recess. "Yes, dear. The doctor said no more grease for this old geezer." She draped an arm over Travis's shoulder and gave him a playful peck against his receding hairline. Looking back at Mercedes, she added, "But I'm sure you knew that, seeing as how you keep up with his well-being and all."

Mercedes wanted to leap across the space between them and tear the woman's hair from her scalp in thick handfuls. But damn it, Nelda was right. She hadn't looked out for her daddy's health since…well, not since the day she'd walked away from this town. She should be ashamed of herself. Instead, she lifted her chin and pegged Nelda with her most evil glare. Before she could open her mouth to unleash the devil himself, Darlene shoved another cookie in front of her face and grabbed her wrist.

"Come on, sis." She dragged Mercedes roughly across the kitchen and out the back door. "Jesus, could you be any bigger of a bitch?"

"She started it." Mercedes knew she sounded like a

petulant teen but couldn't stop herself. "Where the hell does she get off taking over like she owns the damn place?"

Darlene didn't let loose her biting grasp until they were several yards away from the house. "You're being ridiculous and immature. Daddy is happier than I've seen him in years." She led the way toward the corral, her short copper curls whisking against the light breeze.

Mercedes kicked at a few rocks in her path, regretting her decision to come back. Things were already going downhill. First, she fell on her ass in front of her high-school crush, and then she couldn't even one-up an old bat like Nelda. She was losing her touch, damn it. "She's not right for him. For crying out loud, she giggled like a five-year-old."

"I don't give a crap if she howls at the full moon or runs naked in the rain, if she makes him happy, I'm all for it." Darlene stopped and squeezed Mercedes's hand. "She's good for him, and she's good to him. Please don't mess up his happiness."

The words ran cold fingers down Mercedes's spine. Was that what she was doing? Would she be swiping away any shard of happiness her father had finally gained after all these years of being alone? God, was she really such a self-centered bitch?

Mercedes pulled her hand from Darlene's none-too-gentle grasp. "I'll try. Is that good enough?"

Darlene's lip lifted in one corner. "Yeah, that'll do…for now." She started toward the corral again.

Mercedes turned her face to greet a light rush of air. The smell of horses and manure as well as fresh-cut hay met her like a runaway train. "Sheesh," she snarled, her nose twitching as she followed Darlene to the arena. "How the hell can you stand this fucking rank odor every day of your life?"

"Lord have mercy, you actually eat and kiss with that mouth? Keep up that trash talk and I'll be breaking out the lye soap." Darlene pulled herself onto the bottom rung of the split-rail fence.

Mercedes did the same and her breath caught as she spotted a figure closing in on them from the opposite side like a warrior princess on a war horse. Her tight legs hung on either side of the mare's massive body, her posture upright and sure as she put the animal through its paces.

"We're training cutting horses and barrel racers," Darlene explained. "Syd's got a good hand with horses, real gentle but knows how to make them respond to every command."

Mercedes watched, mesmerized. *Whoa, baby.* Sydney Campbell looked spectacular on a horse, and as for her hands, well, who could argue with the facts. Mercedes's memories were as vivid today as they had been all those years ago, when she'd waited for the phone call that never came. Hadn't she come screaming beneath those hands on more occasions than she cared to remember?

"She's hot, ain't she?" Darlene whispered from beside her. "And single."

Mercedes shook her head, but her mind slammed her back against that oak tree, with Syd hovering over her taking what she wanted. Way too much adrenaline pumped through her veins as she remembered Syd's tongue pushing between her lips to explore. An explosion of emotion took root and burst out in a moan she stifled immediately. Her body had quaked with the same curious need back then, thirteen years ago. She'd tried to push Syd off, shoving at her chest, demanding, "Get the fuck off me, you smelly-ass freak."

Syd's words came back to her. "I would, if I thought you wanted me to. The quiver in your voice says you don't."

Her chocolate brown stare was mesmerizing. She'd

lowered herself onto Mercedes, watching her as she held the sides of her face, keeping her in place for that exploring tongue. Not a single kiss had ever come close to making her body jolt with want the way Syd's did. The moment Syd's mouth covered her own, Mercedes came undone. Syd had been gentle as she kissed her way down Mercedes's neck, into the crook of her halter top, before untying the single knot between her breasts. Slowly, she parted the material to free her to the air, then she curled her tongue around each starving nipple…and her fingers had fumbled with the clasp and zipper of Mercedes's too-tight jeans.

Mercedes couldn't move, could only moan and desperately cling to her. Electrifying tingles shot up and down her legs, mingling against her slick pussy. And then she was free of denim and Syd's face was buried between her legs. She should have been embarrassed, should have stopped the madness, but she'd fallen in lust and she couldn't have stopped that train wreck of emotions if her life had depended on it. With the rush of heat inside her body and her gut coiling into a knot, she'd come screaming Syd's name beneath the full moon.

Mercedes dragged herself out of the memory, her pussy wet and her nipples hard. Those kisses…that fuck, it had been the opening of her sexuality, the confirmation that what she'd suspected all along was true. Syd had proven it with one sweep of her tongue and Mercedes had never had a lover anywhere near as breathtaking. She'd hunted for just that kind of kiss, and just that kind of satisfying fuck ever since.

Watching her now, that back firm and tight, her head high and proud, damn it, Mercedes wanted her again. She wanted Syd's fingers buried deep inside, making her come harder than she'd ever come since those first nights. She blinked hard. Syd hadn't wanted her. She'd only wanted to prove something, and once she had she was done with Mercedes. Just as well. Her future didn't have room for a person like Syd even then, no matter how badly she'd yearned for it.

Mercedes hopped down from the fence, her pussy drenched and burning with need. God, how could she allow Syd to affect her after all this time? Wasn't she above this now? Hadn't she worked her ass off to veer clear of people like Sydney Campbell? "She's single because she's a loser with no future. And sexy or not, she's still nothing more than she was the day I left this odor-reeking place." And no matter how hot, and sexy, or goddamn fuckable Syd was, Mercedes wouldn't waste another second thinking about those awesome nights they'd spent together.

"Come on, there's more to see than a wannabe on a damn stinky-ass horse." She turned her back on the woman who'd used her. "Show me what else has changed around here."

Darlene slid off the fence and walked away with her. "Sorry, sis, there's not a whole lot to see that's any different. You're the only thing around here that's changed."

Chapter Four

Syd carried a bowl of mashed potatoes to the table and skirted around Darlene as she fussed over the centerpiece, a basket of homemade biscuits. She could hear water rushing through the pipes in the bedroom above her head and pictured Mercedes standing beneath the spray, her body bejeweled with droplets.

God, how could she still let the bitch unnerve her like she had that morning at the corral? How did she still possess that kind of power over her after all these years? Why couldn't she forget their time together...forget those glorious fucks that still haunted her dreams? Maybe on Friday night at the carnival she could take some little filly home and fuck her until all thoughts of Mercedes Miller vanished from her mind. Irritated with her weakness, Syd turned sharply and bumped into Darlene, who gave her a knowing smile.

"We saw you training the horse today, Syd. Looked like he was giving you a hard time."

The thought of Mercedes watching her unknowingly sent a quake through Syd's body. Did Mercedes yearn for what could have been? Did seeing Syd still make her pussy drip with need? The need to force Mercedes into submission like she once had during those warm long-ago nights quickened in

Syd's blood. Just one more time…one more touch…one more taste. She knocked away the thoughts and answered Darlene.

"He's been stubborn the last few rides. But I'll bring him around. I always do."

Mercedes lying breathless beneath her flashed through her mind again. She'd brought her around—more than a few times, and what a sweet accomplishment it'd been.

By the time the meal was ready and everyone else had assembled, half an hour had passed without further sounds from the second floor. Syd began to wonder if Mercedes planned to join them at all. Was her own presence that unnerving? Maybe if she left, Miller could enjoy quality time with his daughter, although leaving wasn't an option. Syd loved this family and she'd be damned if she escorted herself out for the likes of Mercedes.

Miller walked to the kitchen door and yelled. "Mercedes, get your hind end down here. Dinner's ready!"

A few minutes later, Darlene burst out laughing and Syd turned to see Mercedes in the doorway, her face covered in green goop, her long wet hair spiraling down her back. She wore gray jogging pants with black stripes down the legs with a matching black T-shirt that hugged the flat of her stomach like a layer of suntan lotion. Syd could remember trailing kisses along the sleek surface of that belly…smiling when Mercedes giggled and wove her fingers through her hair, pulling her up for another heated kiss.

"What the…" Miller glared at his daughter. "You will take that concoction off your face before you sit at this table." His dark tone was like ice picks.

The room went quiet.

Nelda patted his hand. "It's okay, sweetie. We want Mercedes to feel at home, don't we?" When Miller grunted, the smile blossomed on Nelda's face. "What, with that busy career and lack of romance, I'd sit around my house in granny pj's with lime pudding on my face, too." She squeezed Miller's hand, love shining bright in her eyes, triumph obvious in her expression. "I did it for many years."

The smile faded from Mercedes's lips. "This expensive seaweed facial mask has nothing to do with my lack of romance or otherwise. I have better things to do with my time than subject myself to the drama of jealousy and clingy partners."

Syd controlled the urge to stare at her. There was sourness laced in her words. Why was she so scornful? And how was it such a gorgeous thing hadn't been snatched up in the sea of beautiful people in LA? She chuckled inwardly at the answer that leapt to mind. Mercedes was single because she was a rattlesnake—no one could take her bite.

Nelda waved her hand in dismissal. "Yes, who needs companionship when you have all that money and all those fancy clothes? Then again, with your busy schedule I'm sure you don't have time to take advantage of either one. Poor child." She pointed to the spare seat beside Sydney. "There, sweetie. We saved a seat for you."

The glare in Mercedes's eyes was unmistakable as she narrowed her sights on her long-ago lover.

Miller tossed a dishtowel at her. "Take it off. Now."

Mercedes sighed but did as instructed, scrubbing at the mess until her olive skin was unveiled. "The dusty air is clogging my pores. And while I'm sure you're all used to that type of torment on your sensitive flesh, I choose not to age before my time." She dared a quick look at Syd, then sat down and turned her attention to the empty plate in front of her.

"Shall we say the prayer before we begin?" Nelda reached for Miller's hand and pulled it on top of the table. "Honey, will you do the honors?"

Everyone joined hands except Mercedes. She took

Darlene's, but kept her right hand firmly in her lap, refusing to touch Syd. Grinning, Syd reached across and pulled the balled fist up onto the tabletop. Mercedes jerked back, but Syd held tight, squeezing those delicate fingers as Miller prayed aloud.

"Heavenly Father, we thank you for the food you've put before us. Thank you for bringing my baby back, if only for a short time. And thank you for the wonderful woman you've brought into my life. Amen."

As soon as the last syllable was out of his mouth, Mercedes tugged her hand from Syd's grasp.

"Aw, honey, that was sweet of you." Nelda leaned over and placed a kiss against Miller's cheek. "You're the most wonderful man I know. Having you in my life is a true blessing."

Mercedes snorted.

Miller gave her a hard stare.

Nelda picked up the bowl of mashed potatoes and handed them to Mercedes. "Here, sweetie, I want you to go first. You look like you're starving yourself with that skinny waist and flat butt. This'll put some meat on those bones."

Darlene burst out laughing.

Mercedes glared. "No, thank you. I work too hard to keep my heart healthy and my waist trim. And I *don't* have a flat butt."

"Oh, I didn't mean any offense, dear. But one would never know with all those loose business clothes you wear." Nelda sat back down and scooped a small spoonful onto her own plate. "Eating properly would also help those small breasts… perk them up. Sure you don't want some?"

Mercedes balled her hands into fists. "Why, you—"

Her father banged his cup against the table. "Best not finish that sentence, little lady."

Darlene was about to slide out of her chair, holding her stomach and slapping the table.

"That's enough, Darlene." Miller's lips quirked as he tried in vain to hide his amusement. "And can't we find something else to talk about?"

"My tits are perky enough, thank you, Nelda. I'm sure you well know it'll be years before they get droopy with age, right?" Mercedes winked, then yanked a biscuit from the basket and began to nibble it as though it was poisoned.

Syd willed the image of Mercedes's nipples out of her mind. She was right. Her breasts were perfect, and soft, and delicious while they hardened on the tip of her tongue. Why couldn't her mind forget? Or her body? Right now, her pussy was dripping just at the thought of Mercedes's body grinding against her own. Even that venomous poison spewing from those lips didn't turn her off.

Sweet Jesus, this was going to be the longest few days of her entire life.

❖

Mercedes was beside herself with rage by the time they cleared the dinner table. Not only did Nelda have a comeback for everything she said, the old goat was actually winning the war. And every grin creeping across Syd's face proved the entire room knew it.

She had to give it to her father's bride-not-to-be, she was damn good at the war of sarcasm. Mercedes found some renewed respect for her. There weren't too many people who could go up against her and still be standing this long into the game, let alone a few steps ahead of her. At least she wasn't engaging in a battle of wits with an unarmed opponent.

But being so close to Syd during dinner was intoxicating. She smelled like Ivory soap and sex…fresh and heated. And even now, with Syd clear across the kitchen, her scent lingered, teasing Mercedes with its musky-sweet aftereffects.

Syd stretched to reach the cabinet above her head, a serving bowl perched in the palm of her hand. The muscles in her arms bunched. Dear God, women weren't supposed to look that edible—enticingly buff in all the perfect places. And she looked completely at home in a place where Mercedes felt like a stranger, where she'd just been treated like a guest when Nelda refused to let her help with the dishes. Without a doubt, she'd put herself in this predicament by abandoning her daddy and sister, by refusing to visit the only home she'd ever known because it held memories she desperately wanted to forget. Would she ever feel at home in this house again? Would the memories ever fade, or be less hurtful? Would she ever get over the scorn of being shunned by Sydney Campbell?

Syd shoved the bowl into place and closed the cabinet door, then turned and caught Mercedes's gaze. Her eyes narrowed for a second as if she were trying to read Mercedes's thoughts. Sucked in by the moment, Mercedes couldn't look away, could only stare and want, knowing full well that her face must be giving away every ounce of her weakness, damn it.

Tremors of heat trickled down her spine, leaving warm goose bumps rising along her skin. How was it possible, after all these years of despising Syd, for her to have the same effect she'd had on Mercedes so many years ago? Those memories never seemed to fade. The images couldn't be wiped from her mind no matter how many women she used for sex. What in the hell was it about Syd that kept her rooted to the past?

When Syd pushed away from the counter, Mercedes snapped present again. Syd swaggered on muscular legs, graceful and confident, all five foot nine inches of her heading directly toward Mercedes. The hair rose on the back of her neck as Syd rounded the back of her chair, then smoothly reached around her and picked up the basket of biscuits. Her fingers brushed against Mercedes's shoulder, and the room swirled out of view. Sweet heavens, but the memories were mind-fucking her all over again. She could damn near feel Syd's fingers trailing along her skin, sinking inside her slick depths, drilling and stretching until she came screaming and out of her mind with saturated pleasure.

No one but Syd had been able to draw her to complete surrender. She hated to admit it, but she needed Syd right this moment, needed her tongue fanning out to lick the heat from her fiery pussy. Mercedes swallowed and drew in a shaky breath as Syd walked back to the sink, where Darlene and Nelda were chatting easily and giggling like they were the best of friends. The sight bothered Mercedes. Hadn't she and Darlene done that a thousand times with their mom right beside them, stopping every now and then to toss suds on each other? How could Darlene have forgotten?

As much as the anger threatened to bubble inside her, the sway of Syd's tight ass drew her out of the danger zone. Fuck, but she had the nicest ass Mercedes had ever laid eyes on. Biteable, that's what it was, and perfectly mounded into muscular buns any sane woman would die to get their hands on. She'd had those delectable cheeks in her hands, had wrapped her legs around their strength and tugged, drawing Syd closer, deeper.

With her mind twisting, Mercedes looked away. Damn it, she had to get a grip on herself before she found herself begging Syd to fuck her…right now she wanted that more than she wanted anything in the world.

"Sweetie, why don't you go get our after-dinner entertainment," Nelda asked, talking to Mercedes's father.

He pushed away from the table and rose. "Good idea." Without another word, he walked out of the kitchen.

"I need to make a quick phone call." Darlene swiped her wet hands across her jeans and practically skipped out of the room.

A quick memory lapsed through Mercedes's mind…of her sister giddy with excitement when Seth Potter used to toss pebbles at their second-story bedroom window. Darlene would kiss Mercedes, a smile dominating her face, right before she eased through the window and escaped down the lattice. God, her daddy would have bellowed if he'd ever known about their secret late-night rendezvous. Darlene had been heartbroken when he'd demanded she never see that "little shithead" again. It was the one and only time Mercedes had been hopelessly happy to see Darlene in trouble. What a difference that her father saw some tiny flaw in his otherwise perfect daughter.

Syd took another serving bowl from the drying rack, once again tortured Mercedes with that slow, deliberate stretch above her head. She watched, unable to help herself; Syd's body was too fucking hot for her not to.

"There." Nelda laid another bowl in the rack and wiped her hands on a dish towel. "Let me go freshen up before we begin." She smiled at Mercedes, who didn't offer the same in return, then left the room, leaving her alone with the object of her hatred—and her infatuation.

"So, tell me what you've been up to all these years," Syd said over her shoulder.

Mercedes let her gaze slide down her back, over that tight ass, down those lean legs, then almost gasped when she realized Syd had turned to look at her. *Busted.* "Like you don't already know where my life and career have carried me. I'm sure my daddy hasn't spared one little detail."

"True…he has bored us on more than one occasion."

Mercedes bit back her gasp, too amused by Syd's sarcasm to allow such a sound to escape her. "Well, considering having a real career is above you, and far out of reach for someone like yourself, I can well imagine it was boring chatter. Hard to keep up when you don't understand a damn thing someone's talking about, huh?"

She knew she should be ashamed for saying such a thing. Syd had lost a lot, starting with the death of her father, ending with a slap in the face when the will announced he was handing over her entire world, the ranch she so desperately wanted, to her no-good brother. Her daddy had filled her in on the details, how he'd put her to work and how she'd outworked every ranch hand on the spread. While it was sad what Syd had lost, it wasn't Mercedes's problem, nor could she find pity when Syd had decided to stay in this hick town instead of getting the hell out and making a real life for herself.

Syd turned slowly, the dishtowel poised over a pan. The expression on her face was void of hurt; instead, was packed full of amusement. "Damn, you haven't changed a bit. I always knew you were pretty self-centered, but until this very moment, I never truly knew just how much."

"What the hell does that mean?" Mercedes rose from her chair and crossed the room to the sink in four single steps. "Don't you dare presume to know anything about me, or what I've done to achieve my goals."

Those eyes, dark and daring, slid down Mercedes's body, licking her flesh with every centimeter of their sickeningly slow descent. "I know enough, trust me, enough to know I don't want to know anymore."

"Fuck you." Mercedes slammed her hand on her hip, feeling foolish for some reason. Her mind was still back in those woods, yet her body was definitely in the heated vicinity of Sydney Campbell. Her pulsing pussy was living proof of that.

"Been there, done that," Syd taunted slowly, "don't wish to venture down that path ever again."

She turned her attention back to the dish rack, leaving Mercedes fuming and desperately wanting to fling herself in Syd's arms for a kiss, for a fuck, for anything Syd would oblige her with. What the fuck was wrong with her? Shouldn't she tear Syd down to size with a few callous words, then storm out of the room, away from any further conversation, and having the last word? Why wasn't she?

Before she could unleash a single word, Syd turned to face her. "Why are you even here? It's obvious you can't stand Nelda, a woman who hasn't done anything to you. You've been downright rude to her from the second you set foot back on this ranch." Syd's lips curled in distaste. "They love each other. Why don't you go on back home and leave us all the hell alone?"

Mercedes chuckled, anger ripping at her gut. "What in the hell do you know about love?"

"Far more than you. Enough to know you're nothing more than a jealous twat who's acting like a spoiled brat 'cause she's not getting her way."

Mercedes scoffed and took a step back, the words like a slap in the face. But God, how true they were, and worse, Mercedes knew she wouldn't change a thing. She was hell-bent to end this farce of a wedding no matter what Syd thought of her. "Nelda is nothing more than a gold digger, and my father must be pretty desperate to pick a woman like her."

Syd laid the pan down, the glare on her face holding Mercedes in check. She took a step closer, towering over Mercedes like a gentle, buff giant. When her breath feathered against Mercedes's cheek, Mercedes couldn't help but close her eyes briefly, desperate for those soft lips to press against her own.

"He's not desperate," Syd said. "He's lonely. Don't let that deranged little brain of yours think anything else."

Mercedes couldn't utter a word while she focused on the tiny black chips that dotted Syd's irises, and her lashes drooping heavily from her lids, the slight signs of crow's feet gathering around her eyes looked damn sexy. Syd had aged well, despite the fact that she'd probably never used any type of facial creams, let alone moisturizers or sun block. Mercedes heard her draw in a heaping breath.

"You have some nerve coming back here after all this time acting like a spoiled rich kid, stomping your feet and making demands. Who the hell do you think you are, and what the hell is your problem? You wanted out of this 'hick' town and you got out. Go on back to your precious city lights and leave your daddy the hell alone."

Mercedes felt her nose flare—felt the anger traveling from her toes, streaking a path up her legs, and bunching in her stomach. She ground her teeth and balled her fists. "My precious city lights make me money. My precious city lights have given me a better life than this rank place could have ever given me. You could have done the same…you could have made something of yourself, instead of staying here to wallow in your self-pity." She held her head high. "Besides, hot sex is in those city lights, darling."

The sexiest grin Mercedes had ever seen spread across those inviting lips. "Yep, just that, nothing more than sex. 'Cause no one in their right mind would keep your ass for long."

Mercedes clamped her teeth together, the sound loud against the deathly quiet surroundings, but before she could react, Syd charged on.

"Your city lights made you heartless. I'll take my calm ranch over your whirlwind of a life any day of the week. And I didn't stay behind to sulk in self-pity." As if there were any room left between them, Syd took another step toward Mercedes. "I stayed behind to watch over my family...your family."

Mercedes jumped as she heard someone clear his throat behind her. Heat prickling her cheeks, she spun around.

Her father held up a Scrabble game. "Since you all have been so *free* with your vocabulary tonight, thought we could put it to good use."

CHAPTER FIVE

Syd tossed the dishtowel on the counter as if the heated conversation hadn't happened at all. "I'm game. But don't forgot the butt-kicking you got the last time."

Everyone piled around the table except Mercedes. She'd be damned if she'd torture herself for another second drenched in Sydney's odor, especially after all the things just said between them. Fuck Sydney Campbell. Besides, her mind was already filled to the brink with erotic memories...there wasn't room for more.

"Aren't you going to play, sweetheart?" Nelda motioned to the empty chair beside Syd. "You being a college graduate and all, figured you could teach us some new words."

That giggle started again, grating Mercedes's nerves beyond repair. She shook her head, reached for her glass, and downed her iced tea. "I think I'll call it a night. This girl needs her beauty sleep. I detest bags under my eyes, though I see you've done wonders with yours."

Ignoring the cut-down, Nelda opened the Scrabble box. "Oh, that's too bad. I was hoping you could give Syd more of a challenge than she gets from the likes of us dumb folk." She grinned though she kept her sights trained on the tiles being passed out before her. "She's the champion around here. Smart as a whip, that one."

Mercedes bit her bottom lip to keep from doubling over with laughter. Sydney Campbell, the champion of Scrabble? The thought was too hilarious. "Syd will have to remain the champ, I'm afraid. I'd hate to take her title."

Syd chuckled in that low rumble that said Mercedes was full of shit, the one that sent swirls of need through her body.

"What are you snickering at?" Mercedes set her glass aside and leaned against the counter.

Syd's eyes slowly lifted from Mercedes's breasts to her face. "Just wondering how big your college was…if it was large enough to fit your ego."

Mercedes ran the tip of her tongue roughly along her teeth to control her growl. Sydney was the last woman she'd allow to get under her skin, even though the wetness soaking her thong was a clear indication she was in far deeper than she dared admit. "Are you challenging me? To Scrabble? Come on, you can't be serious. I've memorized more words in the past year than you've known all your life."

"Then what are you afraid of?"

Mercedes stared at the top of Syd's head for several seconds, then let her gaze stroll down lean arms. Sexy as hell but dumb as a rock, obviously. The ranch hand seriously thought she could beat *her* at a fucking word game? Oh, this was too tantalizing to pass up. "Deal me in."

Mercedes filled her glass with iced tea, then made her way to the table. She deliberately took the empty chair next to Syd, if for no other reason than to aggravate her with her closeness. Heaven knew Syd's was causing an inferno in Mercedes right now…in anger and in pure, unadulterated need for sex. As she scooted her chair under the table, her leg touched Syd's. Though heat rose immediately, her anger pecked it right back down.

She gave Syd a glare. "Do you mind?"

Syd grinned and didn't bother moving, so Mercedes slid her chair over...not nearly far enough away, however. She needed out of this room, out of this house, and out of this fucking town.

Jesus, could this game go any slower?

Round after round, tile after tile, they played. Darlene was the first opponent out, followed closely by her daddy. Nelda was holding strong with her little four- and five-letter combinations and Mercedes had to admit she was more than impressed with Syd. Maybe she'd actually read something other than a "how to birth a colt" manual after all. However, Mercedes was winning by a landslide and couldn't keep the smile off her face.

When the last tiles were counted, and her score was double Nelda's and higher than Syd's by a hundred points, Mercedes leaned back and stretched. "That was fun. I haven't played Scrabble in years."

"Oh, it's not over." Nelda scooped the tiles off the board, placed them all in the bag, and shook the contents. "It's the Miller rules. Last two standing go to war."

"War? This isn't Battleship, this is Scrabble, for crying out loud." Mercedes didn't want to spend another hour slam-dunking Syd. It was obvious who the winner would be. That slouchy country hick couldn't come close to beating a sophisticated college graduate. "It's way past my bedtime, but I enjoyed skunking you all." She pushed away from the table, desperate to remove herself from Sydney's warm thigh and delicious scent.

"Scared?" Syd's deep voice was practically a whisper.

Mercedes slowly turned to face her, and regretted the eye contact immediately. Christ on a stick, but she wanted to crawl over Syd's face and pump against her until her hot pussy cooled to a tolerable temperature. She cleared her throat, afraid the quiver in her voice might give away her heated thoughts. "Yeah, as if." She couldn't resist a smirk of satisfaction. "Come on, I beat you fair and square. To save you another ass-whoopin', you can even keep your champ title. Once I'm gone, you'll still be the smartest one at this table."

Syd only stared, her gaze dipping to Mercedes's breasts before lifting to look her square in the eyes again. "Chickenshit."

"Aw, come on, Syd. Let the city girl go get her beauty sleep." Nelda reached out to squeeze Miller's shoulder. "Besides, I'm sure she's plumb out of words since she used half the dictionary already. And if she were to lose…well. Just let her go to bed."

Mercedes sucked her bottom lip between her teeth. "I wouldn't lose."

"I'm sure you wouldn't." Nelda never looked at her, just continued around the table picking up empty glasses and scraping crumbs into her hand. "But if you did, you'd have to mend fences, since that's the usual bet here in the Miller household. And we all know you're philosophically opposed to ruining your expensive manicure."

Mercedes couldn't believe what she was hearing. Nelda was actually challenging her, prodding her to keep playing. "I wouldn't lose."

Nelda placed the glasses on the counter and turned back to Mercedes, her eyes filled with a mix of humor and scorn. "Prove it," she dared her softly.

Mercedes hesitated. She didn't want to give in, but she couldn't bear to walk away like she was afraid. She gave a casual shrug. "Well, it's not like there's anything else to do around here." With a pointed look at Syd, she added, "Besides, there's no city lights here tonight, though I'm more than capable of taking care of that business myself."

She returned to her chair, aware that all eyes were on her, probably trying to figure out what her little comment meant. A quick glance at Syd proved she'd gotten the meaning loud and clear. Her lips were actually parted and her chest rose and fell a little too fast. Mercedes gave her a smug smile and scooted her chair in. When her leg brushed Syd's, the woman had the nerve to rise from the table and make her way around to the other side as though she expected Mercedes would try to see her tiles. *As if.*

Pulling out an empty chair, Syd said, "Wouldn't want you to think I'd cheated…when I beat you."

"Yeah, that's my life's goal…to cheat at Scrabble." Mercedes took the tiles her daddy dealt and lined them up along the rack. They were a lousy assortment, consisting of two vowels, both identical, and it only got worse from there when she saw the dreaded *Z* in her collection.

"Good hand?" Nelda asked innocently as she sat down next to Darlene. "What's the counter bet, Mercedes?"

"No need. I'll waive my counter bet. She won't win." Mercedes looked across the table, took in Syd's sexy as hell expression as she studied her tiles, and said, "You can go first."

"Awesome. Thanks." Syd arranged her tiles, then slowly placed them on the board. "Quidd. Double for the *Q*, equals twenty-six, and double the word since you were so gracious to let me go first, equals fifty-two."

Mercedes narrowed her eyes at the tiles. "That's not a damn word."

"According to Miller rules it is." Syd winked. "Anything to do with horses is allowed. Besides, you should know that word. That's what horses do when they have a toothache or they can't digest—they dribble their feed out partially chewed."

Fuck! Mercedes stared down at her tiles, at the shitty hand she'd been dealt, even with the extra tile the family always used. She wondered if her daddy had intentionally cheated for Syd's sake and dared a glance at him, but nothing in his gaze suggested he was in on such an act. She perused her tiles intently until she found a word she could join to Syd's. "Zulu. Thirteen points, twenty-six with the double-word bonus." This proper noun wouldn't be permitted in official Scrabble, but the Millers imposed their own rules—and penalties.

"Pertaining to the South African tribe and the language they speak. Nice job." Syd replenished her tiles without looking up.

Mercedes stared in shock, not only that Syd knew the meaning, but because it was getting so hot in the room she could barely breathe. She yanked her sights away from Syd and scooped up her replacement tiles.

Syd took another turn, not even the crack of a smile on her face. She was ahead.

Mercedes bit back a growl and lowered her next word to the board. She had a triple score this time, almost closing the gap. "Viper. A venomous snake."

Syd's lips lifted in one corner. "Also a malignant or treacherous person."

Ignoring the comment, Mercedes replaced her tiles. Syd observed her for several long seconds before she arranged her next word. "Cribbing. Total for me, ninety-nine."

"Cribbing's not a damn word, and you know it." Mercedes resisted slamming her hands down on the table. Anger bubbled inside her as she stared back at Syd. Who the fuck was helping her cheat?

"Watch that mouth, baby girl," her father warned.

Syd's dark eyes, full of triumph, glittered back at her. "A wind sucker…a horse who clings to objects with his teeth and sucks air into his stomach. You should know. Your old horse, Sir Galahad, still does it."

Nelda giggled. "You forgot a lot about this ranch, my dear. Looks like Syd's going to keep her title after all." The giggling escalated as she lightly popped her open hand against the table. "I think I want pictures of our little city girl mending those fences tomorrow."

Mercedes didn't give her the satisfaction of even a glance in her direction. She clamped her teeth tightly together and fumed, hating that her thong was now soaked with the most malicious need she'd ever experienced. Before this horrible vacation was over, she was going to fuck Sydney Campbell until there was nothing left but a lifeless husk of tanned skin. And then she would be on her way, with all of her memories nothing more than faded images.

Knowing full well she was going to lose the game, Mercedes took on a different approach to the slaughter. It was one thing to lose, but quite another to lose with grace and style. She'd lose this war Mercedes style. "Daddy, just warning you, I'm about to use a dirty word."

Giving her a knowing smile, he pushed away from the table and ruffled her hair before placing a kiss against her forehead. "That's my baby, and my cue to leave you girls to the battle." Excusing himself, he disappeared through the kitchen door.

Mercedes turned back to the board. "Clit." She arranged her letters to lead from the C in Syd's word. "Slang for clitoris, the female pleasure center, *the* spot, if treated just right…" She licked her lips and briefly closed her eyes. "Mmm…can also bring earth-shattering orgasms."

The room was deathly quiet for several seconds. Mercedes watched Syd's eyes widen, her nostrils flare.

Nelda leaned toward the table and lowered her voice. "I

was quite good at masturbation, too, Mercedes. Comes with the territory of being alone." She lowered her voice another notch. "I had a vibrator…a pink one."

Not quite the response Mercedes was looking for, but when Darlene burst out laughing, she couldn't help but share in the moment. Syd coughed and laid out her tiles. Mercedes didn't care anymore about her damn horse words. Watching her squirm and making her sweat out the remainder of the game would be much more satisfying than walking up those stairs the winner. That would teach Syd to mess with her again. As for mending fences…yeah, right. Like that would ever happen.

Syd coughed again. Her throat was so dry even the iced tea made no difference. She kept her gaze averted from Mercedes as she tried to concentrate. Drawing in a calming breath, she resisted riding the chair or creeping her hand between her legs to ease the thumping ache caused by the female anatomy theme. And the way Mercedes kept looking at her, like she was thinking about them fucking.

As the game progressed, the array of words that little witch slapped down consisted of "clit," "hole," "ring," which she emphasized by circling her finger around her nipple, and a few other words Syd would rather not repeat, even in her mind. She was ready to come apart at the seams just envisioning Mercedes with a nipple ring. Was she teasing, or did she really have a ring of silver invitation through those splendid nipples? Holy Mother of God, the thought was too fucking erotic. Syd's mind overflowed with images. She prayed the tiles would run out, desperate to ease the bone-melting throb between her legs.

She needed a cold shower, a late-night dip in Miller's pond—anything, as long as it cooled her inflamed pussy. Mercedes was playing with fire, and if she didn't watch it, she was going to find herself naked, and being fucked, right here on this table. With an audience.

"Overo." Syd announced her newest word and laid her winning tiles against the board. She dared a glance at Darlene who winked, proving, without a doubt, that she knew and sympathized with the agony Syd was in right now. Syd finally dragged her gaze up to meet Mercedes's amused eyes. "The genetic equine coat color pattern."

Mercedes waved her hands. "Yeah, yeah. I'm sure the meaning has something to do with a damn smelly horse, something I don't give a shit about." She placed her hands against the table and pushed away. "That's it, folks. Time to take my beaten ass to bed."

Syd knew what she wanted to do with that fine ass, and "beaten" could very well be part of the fantasy she would enjoy later, but right now she wanted to follow Mercedes up to her bedroom, force her face down across her narrow bed, and fuck her until she pleaded for Syd to let her come. Instead, she scooped up the tiles and tossed them in the bag, desperately needing to be gone from this house.

"See you at five, Mercedes."

"Uh-huh, hold your breath for that. This girlie doesn't rise before the roosters. Ever."

Syd grinned. She'd missed this little hot rod. For a brief moment, she forgot how heartbroken she'd been when Darlene announced that Mercedes was gone. Surely she never had a right to feel shunned. Mercedes had never promised her anything—quite the opposite, actually—yet Syd had thought all they'd shared had sparked something between them. How wrong she'd been. It still didn't stop her from wondering what she could have done differently. Had she been nothing but a summer experiment?

The likelihood didn't settle well in her gut. Mercedes

never missed an opportunity to tell people what she thought. If it wiggled through her mind, it was definitely going to spew from her mouth, and Syd had no doubt that Mercedes must have shared their secrets with others, laughed about her experimentation with college friends.

Syd had been too consumed with lust to worry about anything like that. She'd deliberately omitted common sense from her reasoning, because thinking straight would have demanded the impossible from her...*hands off Mercedes.* Syd would never know why Mercedes left without a simple good-bye. Did it even matter now? She knew it did, but also that she might not like the answer.

"Be down for breakfast at five," she warned Mercedes, "or I'll be helping you up."

The glare Mercedes turned on her would have made a grown man shrink in fear. But not Syd. She knew that tiger was clawless...and sounded unimaginable when she was coming, something Syd wanted hopelessly to hear right now. Worse, she had never wished for anything in her life that seemed so impossible to get. For the most part she rolled with the punches. Some hard luck had knocked her to her knees for a while, but somehow, she'd always managed to pick herself up, dust off her jeans, and find a way to keep on going.

That wasn't the case with Mercedes. Always she imagined, and always she questioned what could have been...whether Mercedes had ever once felt anything for her...or if Syd had been nothing more than a sex toy, to be discarded once the novelty wore off. Even after all these years, Mercedes held a part of her that brought Syd to her knees with a burning need. How could she take back the control Mercedes had taken from her so long ago?

Syd stole another look at her. Mercedes was saying her good nights to everyone, but her gaze lingered on Syd. Their eyes met and held far longer than should have been allowed for two people who were supposed to despise each other. Syd looked away first, but not before she glimpsed the naked desire in Mercedes's expression. She held herself from jerking back around for just one more look. Was Mercedes playing games once again? Did she think Syd was weak enough to succumb to her charm? Dear God, she was…and she wanted to act on that invitation so bad it made her mind hazy. Mercedes was no longer an inexperienced kid, she was an experienced woman, and damn if she wasn't one of the hottest women Syd had ever had the pleasure of fucking. Spiteful, and damn mouthy, but hot as sin nonetheless.

As Mercedes ascended the stairs, Syd was tempted further to find out just how much Mercedes had learned. She wanted, no, needed, to know. Would fucking her tear down her defenses and bring her to her knees like it once had? Somehow, she knew it would.

With her pussy painfully flaming out of control, Syd turned to Darlene, conscious of Mercedes's gaze on her. "So, sexy," she asked the woman who'd commiserated with her more than once about Mercedes, "you up for a late-night beer?"

Chapter Six

After some much-needed sexual release and a long night of fitful sleep, Syd crept up the Miller's stairs a few minutes past five a.m. Just as she'd expected, she found a sleeping beauty when she slipped into Mercedes's room. In her sleep, Mercedes had pushed the sheets aside and she looked delicious enough to eat encased in designer lingerie. Too bad Syd was about to drench the uppity little tease. That'd teach her to be late for an appointment with the fences on the eastern boundary of the ranch. Or to leave her without as much as a good-bye.

She stood over the bed, watching Mercedes's chest rise and fall, pushing her breasts against the thin fabric of her two-piece pajama set. Would fucking her be anywhere near as satisfying as it had been all those years ago? Syd knew it would…even better. Mercedes was experienced now, and Syd intended to find out just how much she'd learned. But not right now. With a sigh, and a last glimpse of those sleek legs peeking out from beneath the edge of the sheets, she leveled the bucket over Mercedes's sleeping form, and tipped it up.

In a flash of flailing arms, Mercedes darted off the bed. "What the fuck?" she sputtered, wiping her eyes and peering around the room in a panic to find who or what had tried to drown her. Daggers pierced from her sea green eyes as she locked Syd in her sights. "I'm gonna kick your fucking ass!"

As much as Syd wanted to turn and run from the room, she was rooted to the spot by something else flickering in those evil eyes…desire, need, want, mingling like a prairie whirlwind. As fast as the expression appeared, it was gone.

"You fucking pig. You just signed your own death certificate." Mercedes's jaw was clenched, her fists tight by her sides.

"I warned you not to be late for breakfast," Syd said calmly. "I'm leaving in fifteen. I suggest you be outside and ready."

With a low growl, Mercedes charged at her. Syd braced herself for the onslaught, but Mercedes slipped on a puddle of water, arms flailing like a windmill as she tried to keep her balance. Syd reached for her but was too late. Mercedes slid onto her rear end and her breath expelled in a loud grunt. Unable to resist a smile, Syd stared down at her. She could well imagine the rage coursing through her and had no doubt that she was already plotting her revenge. Her head hung, wet ringlets spiraling around her face.

"What the hell's going on in here?" Miller's head poked around the door.

Syd blinked back desire and looked away from the still-slumped fireball. "I had to wake her up." She held up the bucket for his approval.

Mercedes looked up and whined, "Daddy, this witch just about drowned me."

Miller sipped his mug of coffee and nodded toward the bucket, amusement flicking across his features. "You're supposed to use a cup, not a bucket, knucklehead. You could have drowned the poor child." He turned and left the room as if that imaginary slap on the wrist was punishment enough.

Syd gave a slow, lingering wink at the fuming Mercedes, then followed him. "I couldn't find a cup. I looked, swear."

Her voice faded as they made their way down the hall, both of them acting as though Mercedes wasn't soaked like a drowned rat and this behavior was the most natural thing in the world. "I didn't even fill it all the way up," Mercedes heard Syd say as their footsteps continued down the stairs.

Slamming the door shut after them, Mercedes kicked items out of the way as she flounced toward the bathroom. She dragged her soaked lingerie off and toweled herself dry, outraged that Syd thought she had the right to drag her out to do physical labor only two days before the supposed wedding. Not that she was going to allow that to take place. Over her dead body would her daddy put a ring on that woman's finger. Nelda didn't fool her one little bit with her "sweeties" and her home cooking. Mercedes knew what she was after, and not one red cent would that old goat get her hands on. Her daddy had worked way too long, and way too hard, to have that granny gold digger rip it from his grasp.

She pulled on a clean pair of slacks and cotton blouse and was cleaning up the water from the floor when someone rapped softly on her door.

"Go away!"

Darlene stuck her head hesitantly around the corner. "Don't throw anything at me." She entered with two mugs of coffee. "I figured you could use something hot to warm you up."

"That fucking nobody is gonna get it."

"She's only doing her job, sis. Daddy wants the ranch shipshape for the ceremony. Besides, she warned you."

The ceremony. Mercedes blinked. "They're getting married *here*?"

Darlene stared at her. "Just like it said on the invitation."

"Mom will be turning in her grave."

"I think Mom would want Daddy to be happy," Darlene said quietly. "He's been alone for too long. It's not natural for anyone."

"*You're* alone," Mercedes reminded her. "And I don't hear you complaining about missing out on anything special."

Darlene hung her head, but not quickly enough for Mercedes to miss a sheepish smile. Mercedes gasped. "You're dating someone, aren't you? That's what that phone call and giddy skip was all about last night." She went to her sister. "Do tell!"

Darlene sat on the bed and held out the mug to Mercedes. "You can't tell Daddy. Promise me."

Mercedes took the coffee she was offered and wrapped her hands around the warmth of the mug. "I won't, swear. Tell it, tell it."

"I've been seeing Seth Potter."

Mercedes scoffed. "Old man Potter's Seth?"

"The very one."

Their father had hated Seth's dad from the second all that crap happened at the eventing competition. He still swore that Potter had rigged the whole thing, that he paid off the judges. Mercedes rubbed Darlene's arm. She remembered that weekend very well. It'd been one of the few times she'd heard her daddy cuss, an endless string of foul language, some of which she'd never heard before.

"Daddy had a point, Darlene. Our horses were flawless. Potter's weren't."

Darlene nodded. "I know, and trust me, I still think the same thing." She took Mercedes's hand and gave it a squeeze. "But that was back then, and Seth had nothing to do with it. Still, for the life of me, I can't find the blasted nerve to tell Daddy we're dating. He'll blow his stack, I just know it."

"Oh, Darlene. He'd never blame Seth for something his father did."

"You don't see the looks he still gives them both, like he blames them equally."

Mercedes thought hard. If it was one thing her daddy was, it was fair, and she couldn't imagine him taking his hatred out on an innocent person. There had to be another reason why he would shun someone or be downright rude to them. "Are you sure he doesn't know you're seeing Seth?"

Darlene adamantly shook her head. "No way. We've been extremely careful." A light sparkled in her eyes and a smile crept across her lips. "I was going to tell him after the honeymoon. Figured he would be the happiest then."

Mercedes chucked her chin. "Good idea. Now I have to get dressed before the barbarian marches in my room again. Would hate to have to drop-kick her ass." She went to the closet for a brief inspection.

After wading through several outfits, she changed her mind about her attire, and with evil intent, stalked into the bathroom to change into a bathing suit top and a pair of cotton shorts. Syd knew as well as she did there'd be no mending fences for this city girl, especially where this ranch was concerned. Syd could kiss her damn ass while she caught some morning rays, and eat her fucking heart out.

"That loser is going to regret every drop of water she threw on me…every single drop." She tossed open the closet and dug out an old pair of boots. God forbid she would have to wear anything that resembled cowgirl, but she'd be damned if she would ruin a pair of Jimmy Choos to one-up that stupid ranch hand.

"Play fair," Darlene said as Mercedes stuffed her feet into the boots.

Mercedes snorted as she thought of all the ways she could

seek revenge today, of the many pranks she and Darlene used to play on the ranch hands. A few promising ideas came to mind. "This is my game and I'll play it any way I please," she said, following Darlene out the door.

Twenty minutes later, after gathering a few items to help her show Ms. Ranch Master she'd fucked with the wrong Miller, Mercedes entered the barn to find Syd with two horses already saddled. Their saddlebags bulged with only God knew what. Ignoring the way too delicious woman standing beside the horse, Mercedes folded her tote and stuffed it in the saddlebag of the gelding she assumed she'd be riding.

When she looked back up, she caught Syd's stare oozing over her half-naked body, desire firing in those gorgeous eyes.

"Are we riding or what?" Mercedes slowly shifted her weight to the other foot, loving how Syd's eyes widened and watched so intently.

If she played her cards right, maybe she could be fucking Ms. Hottie within the hour instead of watching her bulging muscles hammer nails. There were so many more delicious ways to up a sweat, and right now, Mercedes knew Syd was thinking about the same "exercise" Mercedes was.

Syd tightened her grip on the gelding, almost like she was using him to keep her balance. Poor thing. "Have you lost your mind? You can't wear that out here in the blistering heat."

"I most certainly can, and I am." Mercedes walked in front of the horse, stopping just short of Syd. "Unless, however, you had something else in mind?"

That sexy grin crossed Syd's lips again. "I have lots of things in mind, darling, but not a single one includes you... except mending those fences." Syd turned away and started packing more items into the saddlebags.

Mercedes pursed her lips and gave a slight huff. What

was it going to take to break this woman down…to fuck her? With a deep sigh, dreading the day of riding a damn horse, or spending it with a woman who had it in for her for some damn reason, Mercedes shoved her foot in the stirrup and attempted to hoist herself up. The horse whinnied and started turning. She quickly removed her foot before he took her for a ride she didn't want. "Hold still, you stupid horse."

Sydney moved around to help her. "Here, go to the other side…he doesn't like to…"

Mercedes swatted her hand away and gave her a steely glare. "Get your hands off me. I know how to ride a damn horse."

Syd backed up, hands poised defensively. "Have at it. I was just going to warn you he doesn't like—"

"I said I've got it!" Mercedes shoved her foot back in the stirrup, grabbed the horn, put her other hand at the back of the saddle, and pulled. Again, the horse started turning, this time whipping his tail around to pop her in the face. She released her hold and backed up. "What the fuck is his problem?"

Syd mounted her horse, adjusted her athletic thighs around the beast, and turned him toward the barn doors. "He doesn't like to be mounted from that side, stubborn ass." She kicked her feet against her horse's side and away she went.

Mercedes stared at the gelding, then walked around the front of him to the other side. "Okay, you big, ugly beast. I haven't ridden a horse in years, so bear with me, I might be a bit rusty. If you promise not to toss me in a ditch, I promise not to touch your sensitive side. Deal?" She stuffed her foot in the stirrup and slowly pulled herself up until she was snug in the saddle. "Thank you. Now follow them."

She clicked her tongue and kicked her foot against his sides. The gelding shot forward with a graceful glide. The feel of his power between her legs gave Mercedes a thrill, something she hadn't felt since she and Darlene used to race across the hills overlooking the lake where they would swim for hours, swinging across the waters from a rope until they dropped into the depths, splashing and having the time of their life. Damn, where had those days gone? Where had her childhood gone?

As she looked out over the vast, drying land, she suddenly missed something about her surroundings. The thought shocked her. She'd never missed a single thing on this ranch, ever. She'd always hated the heat, yet now her skin welcomed the warmth, almost soaking in the rays as if every pore was starved for its nutrition. She'd always despised the ugly, brown grass that emerged over summer, but for some reason it didn't look so drab right now. Actually, quite the opposite. LA didn't offer such freedom to roam. Everything was cramped, and crowded, but here she had three hundred acres she could race across instead of the three feet of concrete that took her from her condo to her car, or the acre of cement that she crossed to get from her parking spot at work to the security gates.

A light breeze teased her body. The odor wasn't quite as potent here as it was closer to the stables. Los Angeles smelled of fumes and toxins. Though she'd become accustomed to the stench over time, right now, she wanted to inhale until she passed out. Mercedes reminded herself that she had the perfect condo, and nothing but designer suits and chic fashionable clothes in her closet. She lived life in a courtroom or in the lab, with a full caseload occupying her analytical mind, and quick fucks on the side when her sexual cravings needed satisfying. No matter how far she strayed from work, work was always on her mind. The thought that she might miss some tiny detail that might make or break a case, or overlook one key element that might put away an innocent person, or worse, set a serial killer free, drove her insane.

Mercedes frowned as she suddenly realized she hadn't

thought about work, or all those cases waiting on her desk, in, what, twenty-four hours? What a rarity that was…and welcoming. It actually felt great to have a free mind, to rid her thoughts of the ugly, sinful people who seemed to dominate her life day in and day out. She slowed the horse when she saw Syd dropping down to examine a cracked section of fencing along the eastern side of the ranch. She was so graceful, and completely at ease, Mercedes had to admit, she could see why her daddy depended on this woman. She was loyal and dedicated, and that meant everything in the world to him.

Mercedes pulled alongside the other horse and dismounted. Tilting her face toward the sunny sky, she sighed. "God, this feels good. Tanning beds are the closest thing I get to sunshine." She looked back at Syd. "Oh, sorry, I bet you don't even know what a tanning bed is, you being out here in the sticks and all."

She hated the words as soon as they escaped. Couldn't she just go an hour without being such a bitch? No. she couldn't. Ms. Ranch hand needed to be taught a lesson—needed to be reminded which Miller she'd fucked with, more than once.

When Syd glanced up, Mercedes gave her a fuck you grin, then walked back to the horses. Making sure Syd wasn't watching, she pulled two Ziploc baggies out of her tote bag, one with ice cubes and the other with worms she'd confiscated from the fishing bait container on the back porch. She ambled over to Syd's horse and withdrew her coffee thermos, unsealed the lid, and dumped the ice inside. That should be a start to her morning of "get even" tricks. Ranchers drank hot coffee all day, swore it kept them from overheating. She'd soon see how Syd liked drinking cold caffeine for her morning jolt.

Mercedes stuffed the empty bag into her front pocket, then went in search of Syd's lunch. She found a sandwich, pulled the plastic back, separated the bread to see a thick, tasty ham creation with lettuce and tomatoes. With a quick glance to make sure Syd was still occupied with her chore, she placed the worms inside, then went back to her horse, ready to begin the next part of her plan, that of making Syd stare at her half-naked flesh.

"Hey, chickenshit, why don't you come over here and help me get these boards off?"

"Chickenshit? Whatever! I've already mended my fair share of broken boards in my lifetime." Mercedes tugged a blanket from the side of the horse. "Besides, that's your job, not mine. I have a cushy job, with great benefits."

"Yeah, well, last time I checked we weren't in a damn city. And in case you forgot, you lost a bet. Now get your bony ass over here and get your day started. Or are you scared?"

Mercedes glared at her, never one to turn down a dare or let anyone tell her she was a slack-ass. "Scared of what? A hammer, nails, and a fucking wooden board?"

Syd's grin stretched over white even teeth. God, Mercedes wanted to lick those lips, slip her tongue inside Syd's mouth, then fling herself into those strong arms.

"I think you need your mouth washed out," Syd said. "All you had to say was that you were scared of getting a splinter in those delicate, no...working hands."

Oh, that fucking loser. How dared she compare Mercedes's job to a damn rancher's? Mercedes let the blanket drop from her fingers, stalked over to Syd, and jerked the hammer from her hands. "Yeah, you and what damn army? Get out of my frigging way."

Over an hour later, she was still kicking rotted wood, hammering up new boards, and traveling down the length of the fence, all with Syd dangerously close behind her. Even through the heat of the day, the heat from Syd was unmistakable... daring and wild.

"You need to put a shirt on." Her tone was disinterested, as though she'd only just noticed the flesh on display, and then just for health reasons. "You're already getting pink."

Mercedes turned around and regretted immediately that she'd done so. Syd shucked off her shirt and held it out to her. Mercedes closed her eyes but she couldn't shut off the image of Syd: beautifully toned, tanned arms; delicate lines of muscles coursing up her bicep. *Kill me now!* The thought scurried through her mind as she licked her salty lips in an attempt not to leap into those arms and fuck her right there beneath the sweltering sun.

"Thanks, but no thanks. I need a little tan." She wouldn't dare admit that her skin already felt like a sheet of leather and was sensitive even to the light breeze, or that she was sporting several blisters on her hands. She'd be damned if she let Sydney Campbell see her sweat, or falter in any way.

"Okay, but you're not going to think that tomorrow when you can't move."

Mercedes waved her hand in dismissal. "You should have thought about that before you dragged me out here. Weren't you expecting me to work?"

"You? Never." Syd withdrew her offering and tossed it over the back of the horse, which had followed them obediently.

Mercedes's horse had wandered off almost as soon as Mercedes released him. Damn it, even the horse she rode had a mind of his own...and now she'd have to go fetch him if she wanted a ride back to the house.

Thirty minutes later, she could barely swing the hammer. Her arms felt like rubber and her hands felt like someone had sliced them open with a butter knife. Sweat rolled over her skin, making a glossy sheen for the sun to attack even more than it already was. When she turned and found Syd by her side, Mercedes almost gasped out loud. "What?" She pushed her loose hair from her face with the back of her hand. "Am I not doing it right, oh master ranch hand?"

Syd held the shirt out insistently. "Put it on."

"I don't want the damn shirt." *Liar!* She longed to grab the garment and hold it close to inhale Syd's aroma.

"Now," Syd barked. "Your back and shoulders are red as fire."

Mercedes huffed—only for show, since she desperately wanted something covering her blistering skin. She was going to look like a lobster by the time she got back to the ranch, and the wedding was only two days away. If it went ahead she was going to look like a walking, flaming cherry for all to see.

As she reached out to take the shirt, Syd grabbed her wrist and turned her palm up. "That's what I thought. Why didn't you tell me your hands were hurting?" She pulled Mercedes toward the horse and unstrapped the saddlebags.

"If they were, I might have." Mercedes tugged her wrist to no avail.

"These are going to get infected if you don't get some ointment on them." Syd withdrew a white tube, clenched it between her teeth, and unscrewed the cap.

"Yeah, well...ouch!" Mercedes pulled against the tight grip as Syd smeared the gel over her raw flesh.

"You had a splinter. Damn stubborn-ass woman. I have extra pairs of gloves in the bag."

Mercedes wouldn't grace her with a response. Right now, she was held captive in Syd's power. Fuck. She wanted to slick her tongue against Syd's thin lips and slide inside that inviting mouth. When Syd let go of her hand, she felt disconnected somehow. But her palms felt cool where seconds ago they were burning. She looked up into Syd's eyes, an automatic *thank you* trembling on her lips. But the emotion she saw in those dark depths made the words evaporate. Mercedes knew that look. She'd seen it a long time ago and it had mystified her then, too. Far from being disconnected, she felt closer suddenly, and before she could stop herself, she touched Syd's hand.

Tingles pierced her skin even through painful blisters and ointment, not from sexual tension, but from a past that was strong enough to hold her captive thirteen years later. She had given herself to Syd, not so willingly at first, but without hesitation thereafter. Syd held a tender part of her that Mercedes didn't regret giving. She'd trusted her.

Their gazes locked, and Mercedes felt her defenses crumble. The old hurt caused by so many sleepless nights, waiting for Syd to call, vanished, and all that remained was the connection they'd created beneath the watchful eye of the moon and a sprawling oak tree. She took a step closer, wanting, no, needing to feel those lips against her own.

Syd inhaled and the spell was broken.

Mercedes instantly stepped back, terrified of the pull Syd still had over her. "I don't need your gloves," she said weakly. "Or your help."

Syd didn't answer. She jerked her hand away and stomped back to her horse.

Chapter Seven

S yd found a shaded spot under a large tree for their lunch and spread out the blanket. This was her favorite spot on the entire ranch. The mountains loomed like gentle giants directly in front of them; the large pines lining the property created a protective barrier of massive timbers. Having Mercedes there with her made it seem a little more special for some reason. Without once looking at Mercedes, she unpacked the picnic lunch from the saddlebags and lowered herself onto the blanket, dangerously close to the woman who'd ripped all rational thought from her mind throughout the morning.

Watching that slender body bending and straining, the skin pinkening beneath the sun's dangerous rays, had made her weak with need, even wetter with want. How such a thing was possible, she still didn't know, considering the bitch had left her at the beginning of their relationship without a word of good-bye.

Syd had stopped wondering a long time ago where in the hell she'd gone so horribly wrong that she was treated like dirt. As the years went by without a word from Mercedes, she'd finally concluded that timing was the problem. Mercedes was too young and self-centered to get involved, and Syd had her own problems, too, in those days.

With her mother dying of cancer, her father had practically abandoned them all with his need to drink away the pain. Her brother wasn't much help, not that he ever was, but it would have been comforting to have his support, something she'd never known. He'd left town within six months of bankrupting the ranch he'd undeservingly inherited from their father. Who could blame him? He was practically shunned by the whole town. His bar room brawls and taste for married women didn't sit well with anyone, especially after he didn't have a pot to piss in, or the money to buy his way out of jail.

Syd thought about him often but knew she'd never see or hear from him again. Saddest part was, she couldn't care anymore. What mattered was that she'd lifted herself up and started all over, thanks to Miller, who had seen her desperation and given her a chance to prove herself. She'd done just that and wanted nothing more than to be running her very own ranch a few years from now.

It was funny how things worked the way they did. Everything happened for a reason. She almost snorted out loud remembering how badly she'd wanted to tame the rancher's daughter, how crazy she was to ever get involved with the little vixen. She'd known it all along, but she couldn't help herself. Was it sick of her to still want Mercedes? Didn't she deserve some answers from her? Yet, asking those long-thought-about questions would show her weaknesses and vulnerabilities to the devil herself. Worse, it would give Mercedes that cutting edge over her.

Desperate for liquid, and a reason to keep her hands busy, Syd uncapped her thermos. Right now, all she had to do was turn and she could tower over Mercedes, pin her down, and fuck her beneath the cover of the branches like the old days. Just as she lifted the thermos, she heard Mercedes's intake of breath. The sound sent a spark of fire right to Syd's pussy at the same time ice-cold coffee filled her mouth. She rolled to the side and spewed the nasty liquid from her mouth, a smile tugging the edges of her lips. How could she be so stupid? She should have known there was no way a woman like Mercedes Miller would let her wake-up call pass without seeking some kind of revenge.

A smile teetered on the witch's lips as Syd wiped her mouth with the back of her hand. "I considered stopping you." Mercedes lowered her lashes. She looked almost genuine, if not for the way she was chewing her bottom lip as if to halt a bout of laughter.

Syd wanted to wipe the grin right off the little witch's face, then plunge her fingers so far inside Mercedes, she'd yelp in surprise. Restraining herself, she said, "Yeah, I just bet you did. You shouldn't have overloaded your brain with such a difficult decision." She poured the remaining coffee away and tossed the thermos toward the grazing horses. "Are there any more surprises I should know about?"

Though Mercedes casually shook her head, Syd was more than sure her pranks were far from over. Mercedes didn't fight fair. She never had. Syd dug around in the picnic bag and found a bottle of water. As she drank from it, her mind strayed to the first time they'd ever met. Syd was nineteen and had already started making a name for herself on the Western events circuit in Colorado. Mercedes was a few years younger.

Perched like a sun goddess across the hood of her daddy's Ford pickup while a horse competition went on around her, she drew looks from every passing cowboy. Syd remembered the moment like it happened only yesterday, how Mercedes looked like she owned the damn place. That white halter top left little to the imagination and hadn't helped Syd concentrate on her roping event. She already knew her sexuality and had acted upon it enough times to know she wanted to practice everything she'd learned on the little twat with her nose to the sky. The Daisy Dukes Mercedes sported were just low enough to show curvy thighs, yet high enough to tease every man walking by...as well as Syd.

Travis Miller would have cut the balls off any man who dared stop within two feet of his truck. They could look, but bless their hearts if they dared touch. And the whole town knew it. But there'd been something about Mercedes, something Syd had never been able to put her finger on...something so intense that it made her dare lay her hands on her, only a few weeks later. She knew there could be repercussions, but she didn't care. By then all she could think about was that little temptress.

God rest her dad's soul, but it was during a trip to Miller's ranch with him to purchase a gelding that Syd got the chance to wander around the ranch. And there she was, curled beneath that damn oak tree, book poised against her bent knees. She was the most breathtaking thing Syd had ever seen—and she'd stolen a kiss and gotten slapped. What Mercedes couldn't hide was her curiosity, and her shock that Syd had dared do such a thing. But she'd liked it, Syd could tell. And when Syd eventually came back for more, Mercedes had given her more.

Syd hadn't expected to want her just as badly now. She shook her head, sick that she felt this way. There wasn't a woman alive who could hold this much power over her. Syd had relationships from time to time, if they could even be called "relationships." Taking some cute little filly home when her cravings took control was her norm, and each and every one of them knew it. She never made promises, and they expected nothing in return. It was safe that way. She was always in control, well, almost always. Mercedes had taken quite a chunk—then, and now.

How the hell had Mercedes regained such control after only a few hours? Or had she held it this whole time? All these years? With a knot forming in her stomach, Syd knew the answer. Every time she was with Mercedes, she could feel her control slipping away. Mercedes possessed her in ways she could not explain, invading her mind and engulfing her body. That was just an undeniable fact.

"So, what's next, boss?" Mercedes lay back on the blanket. The shirt Syd had given her slid open to reveal her covered breasts.

Syd knew what her nipples looked like beneath the hot pink fabric of her bikini top, how they swelled to hardened peaks when they were sucked between her teeth. And then she saw it, the defined lines of a ring. Sweet heavens above, Mercedes was sporting a nipple ring! Syd dared a glance at the other breast and found a matching circle. Lust poured over her, hotter than any Colorado sky. She tore her gaze away as need flowed through her like molten lead.

"What's next?" Syd repeated, concentrating on keeping her voice steady. "Same ol' thing until we reach the edge of the woods. Then we'll call it a day."

Mercedes leaned up on her elbows to study her. "Wanna see them?"

Syd looked down at her, feigning puzzlement. "See what?"

Mercedes laughed. "Like we both don't know you've been staring at my tits for the past two minutes."

At this moment Syd wanted to see those damn nipples more than she wanted to own her own ranch. Then she wanted to chew on them, see if the sensitivity was heightened by the rings, as she'd heard. She felt a trickle of sweat run down her spine as Mercedes reached for the knot at the nape of her neck.

"Not like you don't know what they look like, right?" The bathing suit went limp against Mercedes's chest, still covering what Syd desperately wanted to see.

Syd looked away and grabbed the sandwich bag. She removed the contents before she could change her mind, before she could look back to see if Mercedes beautiful breasts would be revealed for her gaze. She tossed the sandwich labeled bologna to Mercedes, then unwrapped her own.

"You sure you don't wanna peek?"

"Positive. I've seen plenty of nipple rings. Don't do anything for me." She nodded toward the sandwich. "Eat. It's going to get hotter before we're done, and you'll need your energy."

She put the sandwich to her mouth and just as her teeth sank into the fresh bread, she felt something wiggle against her lips.

Mercedes snickered. "Yummy-fresh worms for your dining pleasure."

Syd fumed as she withdrew the sandwich from her mouth to witness several worms peeking from between the folds of the bread. With a growl, she threw it aside and rose from the blanket. She towered over Mercedes for several agonizing seconds before grabbing her arm and hoisting her forward. When Mercedes slammed against her chest, it was all Syd could do not to plunge her tongue between those luscious lips like she'd wanted to do when Mercedes reached out and touched her hand, mesmerizing her with that easy stare. And from the shock and arousal on Mercedes's face, she wanted the same thing.

Syd ground her teeth almost hard enough to crack them. "My coffee is one thing, but my lunch is quite another. Take off my damn shirt, you inconsiderate twat."

She knew her mistake as soon as those sea green eyes

flashed. Mercedes slowly shucked off Syd's shirt at the same time her bathing suit top fell around her hips. Beautiful olive breasts met Syd's gaze, tiny silver rings pierced through pert nipples. *God, strike me dead now and put me out of my misery.* Syd's tongue danced behind her lips as she stared at the teasing circles of stainless steel.

Mercedes watched her, the tip of her tongue moistening the edge of her lips. "You can blink now."

The sound of her voice yanked Syd back to sanity. She tugged her shirt from Mercedes's grasp and slowly bent down, her face dangerously close to those nipples standing at attention. Mercedes's chest rose and fell with shallow breaths. She tilted her head back slightly, expectantly. A smile tricked across Syd's mouth. She bent even closer, letting her breath roll over the upturned face. Their lips almost brushed as Syd spoke.

"If I can't eat my lunch, neither can you." She grabbed Mercedes's sandwich and stepped back, immediately straightening. "You have water in your saddlebag. I suggest you drink it, then get your ass back to work."

Throbbing with need, Syd strode toward her horse and tightened the saddle. Forcing herself to relax, she trotted casually away from the tree once she was on horseback again. After a minute or two, she dug her heels into the gelding's flank and he broke into a gallop. She could feel Mercedes watching, but didn't look back, needing space between herself and the woman she wanted to mount like a derby rider and fuck until she howled like a wolf.

❖

Burning with resentment, Mercedes cleared away the last of the picnic and folded the blanket. Why hadn't she just ripped the sandwich from Syd's grasp like she'd wanted to and ceased the whole revengeful game? How simple would that have been? Jesus, could that woman look any more edible, with sweat trickling over her face and across the subtle curves of her throat as it disappeared into her cleavage? The sight had been teasing Mercedes into a wet ball of need ever since they'd left the ranch house. She'd never wanted to rip a tank top off a woman so badly in her life.

She'd drawn a strange erotic pleasure from watching that sandwich inch toward Syd's lips. Or had she been mesmerized by the lips themselves? God, what the fuck was wrong with her? First, she wanted to fuck Syd. Next, she wanted to rip her a new asshole.

She felt like two completely different personalities were competing inside her. She was unable to keep her thoughts straight if her life depended on it. She wanted Syd, yet despised her. She wanted to fuck her, yet she didn't want Syd to touch her at all. What was wrong with her? And why was she still standing here questioning her confusion and ignorance when she should be racing after Syd, if only to apologize?

Maybe she would change her mind by the time she caught up with Syd, but Mercedes decided she'd been stubborn long enough. Determined to say what needed to be said, if she even knew what that was, she climbed in the saddle and urged the horse into motion. The wind barreled against her chest and stomach as she broke into a gallop, determined to get to the bottom of this malfunction with Syd—if that's what she could gracefully call this. Mercedes knew the problem lay within herself.

She was flat-out being a bitch. No other way around it.

As she veered the horse around an oak tree, she caught sight of a lone calf at the edge of the woods. She slowed down, first looking in the direction Syd had raced off, then back to the calf. With his mother nowhere in sight, she could only assume he was lost, and afraid. She'd felt that emotion more times than she cared to admit. It wasn't a great feeling.

However, the calf was an animal, right? They had instincts. Surely he'd find his way back to his mother without interference. But normally the mothers recognized the sounds their offspring made. Where was the neglectful cow?

"Screw it." Mercedes urged the horse forward once again, her mind already reeling with the things she wanted to say to Syd, all the questions she wanted to ask. But she couldn't stop thinking about the lonely calf. He would die if she left him. Without his mother, he'd starve, and it might be days before anyone found his lifeless little body. She couldn't leave him, she just couldn't do it, no matter how desperate she wanted to smooth things over with Syd.

In frustration, she pulled on the reins and turned back around, a growl rumbling in her chest. Trotting along the edge of the woods, Mercedes couldn't see any sign of the cow. The calf was crying, high-pitched little whines that tore at her heart. She dropped down from the saddle and tied her horse to the nearest tree, then cooed the calf until he finally stopped making that plaintive sound.

As she was soothing him, she heard the unmistakable sounds of mooing coming from deeper into the woods. Following the sounds, she made her way toward a rocky rim that was normally fenced off. The fence had been flattened in the center by a fallen tree and Mercedes struggled over broken branches to reach the rim of a steep crevice. Peering down, she spotted the cow trapped on a rocky section of the slope, unable to get a foothold. She looked weak and helpless, her eyes flashing frantically as she struggled to find a way back to safety and her calf. Mercedes knew she should go after Syd instead of standing here agonizing over the animal's predicament, but she didn't want to ask for help. Syd already thought Mercedes's ranch skills were worthless—everyone did, including her daddy, and she definitely hadn't done anything to prove them wrong.

Did she even care? Poised on the ledge, she realized that she did. Somehow, as a kid, she'd started pretending their opinions didn't concern her. She'd been demoralized because everyone constantly praised Darlene's abilities and scoffed at Mercedes's attempts to be a true rancher's daughter. She'd concluded by the time she got to high school that she could never win. No one took her seriously. So she'd tried to impress them in other ways. She'd been doing that ever since, proving she was a "success." Not that it made any difference. Her determination to leave the ranch behind only made her father and Darlene feel rejected.

She'd never meant for that to happen. Mercedes understood now that she'd scorned their ideas and values because she was trying to show that she didn't give a damn. Her act had soon become a habit and in the end she did stop caring. Only Syd had the power to get past her defenses and make her doubt herself. Only Syd could make her feel uncertain about what she really wanted…and who she really was.

After carefully taking in her surroundings, assessing the mounds of rocks circling the cow and the steep incline down, Mercedes stepped into motion, determined to be the savior. She may have hated this damn ranch, but her daddy had taught her how to be a tough cowgirl, how to keep a level head in the face of danger, and if for no one but him, she was going to get this job done.

She sprang back to the gelding and unstrapped the coil of rope no rancher ever left home without. You never knew when a simple thing like a length of rope could save the day. Today, it was going to save that damn cow's life…she prayed.

Mercedes scrambled back to the rim of the crevice and sorted through broken tree limbs until she found a short but sturdy branch she could use for leverage. She looped her rope around the nearest tree, then tossed the branch down ahead of her and winched herself down, holding tight to both ends of the rope. Her life flashed though her mind as she made the risky descent. This was her home, her ranch, her field, and that creature barely mooing down in the crevice was her damn cow, a living being that depended on her. No matter how far away from home she'd wanted to get, this land was always inside her. The knowledge was shocking, yet gratifying at the same time. What was she doing in LA, a place she couldn't walk barefoot in her own front yard, a place where neighbors barely said hello, let alone invited you over for a barbecue?

Dismissing the disturbing thoughts, Mercedes set her mind on the job at hand. The slope deepened, making her footing more difficult. She held on to every bush she could get her hands on, praying they didn't dislodge and send her tumbling ass over feet right into the cow. God forbid she had to be rescued along with the animal. That'd sure prove Syd right.

When she reached the weary cow, she breathed in a sigh of relief and stalled for a minute to access any damage. Thankfully, there were no injuries that she could see. The cow hadn't fallen. She must have wound her way down into the crevice at an easier access point, then tried to make her ascent and trapped herself between the two large boulders Mercedes had just landed between. The way up was tough but not impossible, if she could just get the both of them over the rocky ledge directly ahead.

She spoke gently as she looped an end of the rope around the cow's neck. Too weak to protest, the cow merely snorted. Quickly, Mercedes tied the other end around her waist and walked down the side of the cow. The animal might seem weak now, but would she start rutting or objecting once Mercedes prodded her into motion? Heaven help her if that happened. She would be useless against its massive weight.

No time to turn back now. Using the broken branch as leverage behind the cow's butt, she wedged the other end between the large rocks. With every ounce of strength she possessed, she started winching, lying backward and using her full weight, pulling the ropes tighter as the cow slowly started forward. The tree easily bore both their weights and Mercedes worked the levering branch to boost the cow further. Hearing her calf, and feeling herself finally making progress, the hefty beast seemed to find a surge of strength and heaved herself up, miraculously making it over the first ledge and finding some footing. Mercedes urged her on, pushing with all of her strength, pulling with all her might, and winding in every spare inch of free rope so there was no slack. Her chest felt heavy as she strained, the rope around her waist digging deeper into her flesh. With a growl of pain, she threw the weight of her body backward, and to her amazement, the cow scrambled over the steepest part of the slope and onto a gentler rise.

Mercedes clawed her way up after her and fell to her knees beside the cow, gulping in heavy breaths. Valuable time had passed, and the darkening shadows cast by the tall trees above gave her an eerie, lonely feeling. How long had she been hoisting this damn cow upward? An hour, maybe more? Why hadn't anyone come looking for her? Didn't they care that she hadn't returned home with Syd? Didn't Syd give a shit where she might be?

She gathered her remaining strength, along with a flare of anger, and prodded the cow into motion once again. Not too much farther to go, and even as exhausted as she was, she felt jubilant to have saved some stupid cow—to be reuniting her with her calf. She wound in the excess rope and retied it around her waist, then got to work again, this time pushing the cow from behind without the branch as a lever. Now that the animal had some traction, she was gaining ground independently. It was just as well, Mercedes thought as her arms trembled with strain. They were building momentum, kicking up dust and stones. Mercedes gave one last desperate shove and felt the weight lifted from around her waist as the cow dug into flat ground. They were over the rim! She'd done it!

Mercedes collapsed in a heap beside the cow, spent of energy, almost unable to breathe. Her head spun and all she could hear was the sound of her own raspy panting. When she heard a movement close by, she finally opened her eyes to see a pair of boots, slightly bowed legs, and then tanned, strong arms reaching for her.

With a sob, she allowed Syd to pull her into her grasp and clung tight, letting herself take comfort in that strong embrace.

❖

Stunned, Syd cradled a depleted, crying Mercedes to her chest. "Shh. It's okay, I got you."

She rocked and hated herself for not coming in search of her sooner. She'd half expected Mercedes to follow her, though why, she'd never know. Mercedes wasn't the chasing kind. When she didn't, it only angered her further; made her feel more ignorant than she already was for thinking about the vixen after all these years, or letting her pranks and flirtatious eyes unnerve her.

For over an hour, she'd beat the hell out of every board that needed replaced along the northern fence, determined to jolt Mercedes out of her mind. Instead, all she'd managed to do was hammer her own thumb against fresh wood. Mercedes was still there, deeply embedded in her mind, where she'd been for thirteen restless years, and where she might possibly be after thirteen more.

And now, after witnessing Mercedes shoving a ton of a cow up a steep embankment, using her own weight and strength, determination etched across her strained, beautiful face—well, Syd would never be able to shut her out of her mind, that was for sure.

It was the most breathtaking image of Mercedes she could ever possess, and she knew she'd never be able to erase that particular moment from her consciousness...of Mercedes giving all she had to save something other than herself, giving her entire heart to save a damn cow.

Mercedes sniffled. "Where's the calf?"

"She's nuzzling her tired mama." Syd held her tighter, feeling the heat of Mercedes's naked flesh against her arms and loving every second of it. "You did great."

Damn if Mercedes didn't feel incredible, and perfect, tucked against her body like she'd been tailored to only Syd. Even with Mercedes too weak to move, Syd wanted to lay her down against the ground and make love to her...wanted to taste every inch of her salty flesh while kissing away every silky tear.

Tenderly she untied the rope from around Mercedes's waist, careful to avoid the deep red burns marking her otherwise flawless skin. Then she gently scooped her up and carried her to the waiting horses. Syd lifted her onto the saddle Mercedes would share with her; Syd wasn't willing to let her ride unaided. She fished a bottle of water from the saddlebags and watched Mercedes drink thirstily, water oozing over the rim, down her neck, and cradling in her cleavage.

Syd felt a stab of guilt that she could find the sight of her so sexy after the precious moments she'd just witnessed. To avoid giving herself away, she hitched Mercedes's horse and the cow to her own, then hoisted herself into the saddle behind Mercedes. She slowly led them across the pasture to the lake, the calf following very close behind, not daring to let her mother out of her sight again.

The animals drank greedily while Mercedes leaned against Syd's body like she belonged there. Nothing could feel more natural, and Syd found herself drowning in the moment, wanting these precious seconds never to end. A wrenching sadness overtook her as she thought about Mercedes leaving in a few short days, how fast that time would be upon them. God help her, she didn't want Mercedes to leave.

Without a doubt, she knew that departure was going to break her heart all over again.

❖

It was dusk when they reached the ranch house and Mercedes was too exhausted to protest when Syd carried her indoors and set her gently down on a couch in the living room.

"Oh, sweetie. Look at you, all sunburned." Nelda cantered toward them, her eyes moving from one to the other. "That must burn like the dickens. Forget to wear a shirt? You'd think someone from a big ol' city like LA would have better sense."

"What does LA have to do with anything?" Mercedes retorted, but there was no fight in her voice. "Anyway, I'm from here...*Colorado*, in case you don't remember."

A simple smile crept across Nelda's face. "Yes, dear,

though I wasn't sure if you did." She turned toward Syd, her eyes suddenly fierce. "How could you let this happen? You know better." She waggled her finger.

Her protective tone astonished Mercedes so much, she didn't interrupt.

"Me? Why are you blaming me? She's the stubborn ass who refused to take my shirt." Syd's expression begged for forgiveness. "She wore a bathing suit, for crying out loud."

"I don't want to hear your excuses. You're in charge of this ranch, aren't you?" Nelda strode out of the room but returned quickly with a container of Noxzema. She knelt beside Mercedes and without asking, started gently smoothing the ointment over her raw skin.

Mercedes winced in pain before the balm started cooling her skin.

"Poor child. This should take away your pain in no time." Nelda moved to the other side, stalling long enough to give Syd another dark glare. "Travis is going to be furious with you."

Syd threw her hands up. "This is ridiculous. You can't possibly blame me for her absurd behavior."

"I can, and I am. You should have sent her right back in this house to change into proper clothing."

Syd sighed and sank into the nearest chair. Mercedes dared a glance at her, too overwhelmed with emotions to think coherently right now. Just minutes ago, those arms had held her tight and she'd wanted nothing more than to turn in Syd's grasp and capture those lips. Fuck if she hadn't thought about turning completely in the saddle and pumping against that beefy stomach until an orgasm shattered through her body.

And now, with Syd looking helpless, she wanted her all the more.

Nelda cooed and continued massaging the cream into her

skin. Mercedes sank into the moment, remembering her own mother doing the same thing for her and Darlene. Nelda had mother hands, gentle and caring. Mercedes cringed inside. Dear God, was Nelda really a good person? Would she make her daddy happy? With her heart sinking, she knew the answer. Nelda had already made him a happy man, it was shining bright in his eyes every time he looked at her.

"And you, little lady, should know better as well." Nelda tapped her shoulder, shocking Mercedes with that motherly tone. "I'm more than sure you've sported enough sunburns here on this ranch to know you can't act so foolish under these skies."

Syd smirked and Mercedes resisted the urge to stick out her tongue. Right now, she was too damn tired to care who took the blame. She wanted a hot, scalding bath to ease her throbbing muscles, but that was impossible with her sunburn. All she could look forward to was a cool, stinging shower and a good night's sleep. Fuck! Her bed was soaked, thanks to that all too sexy Syd.

Mercedes closed her eyes and let the day drain from her mind. "I saved a cow." She wasn't sure why she said it, but it sounded pleasant coming from her own lips.

"A cow? Did you say a cow?"

Mercedes opened her eyes to find Nelda hovering over the couch, eyes narrowed. "Yes, a cow. She was stuck at the bottom of the ravine."

"Do what?" Nelda's shriek jarred Mercedes into an upright position. She suddenly felt like she'd been busted playing another prank on one of her daddy's ranch hands. How many times had she been punished for such mischievous acts.

Nelda turned a blazing glare on Syd. "What in God's name were you doing while this poor child was manhandling a cow?"

"Mending the north fences."

"Good Lord save us all, she could have died." Nelda sat down beside Mercedes, staring over her like she'd nearly lost her only born child.

What was up with that? And why was Mercedes suddenly feeling the need to crawl into her lap and cry like a two-year-old?

"That's it. Up the stairs you go, young lady. A soothing bath is what you need, and a long sleep." Nelda gave a pointed look at Syd. "Off with you. We'll deal with this matter first thing in the morning."

Mercedes wasn't surprised to see Syd stand to attention and head out of the house. Poor Syd. She'd have to correct Nelda on a few things tomorrow, but right now, Mercedes was too tired to care, and that bath sounded like heaven.

She allowed Nelda to guide her up the stairs and almost let out the sob still trapped in her throat when she saw that her bed had been dried and made with fresh sheets. God, she should be ashamed of herself for acting the way she had...for being a callous bitch determined to shatter this woman's world.

"Thank you." The word sounded truthful to her own ears. She prayed Nelda heard her sincerity as well.

"No need to thank me, sweetie." Nelda brushed back a strand from her eyes. "Go get that bath and I'll have you some soup ready when you get out." With that, she left Mercedes alone and closed the door behind her.

Only when she was safely behind the locked bathroom door and submerged in neck-deep sudsy water Nelda had carefully adjusted to a mild temperature did Mercedes let her tears loose. She wasn't sure exactly what she was crying for. Guilt. Regret. The aftermath of an adrenaline rush. But it didn't matter. The release felt good and Mercedes felt so relaxed by the time she got out of the water and dried herself off that she could have fallen asleep on the bath mat.

She stumbled into bed and smiled with contentment. For once, someone was looking after her. Mercedes had forgotten how good that felt. After sleeping for several hours, she woke up with a start, convinced she could feel Syd's strong arms around her. She stared around her darkened room in disappointment. She was alone and she could hear voices downstairs. Mercedes thought about going down but she didn't think she had the strength in her legs to walk. She tossed and turned, her skin sensitive and raw and every muscle aching. A carousel of images floated through her mind, vivid pictures of Syd's face, shocked that Mercedes had actually hoisted the beast up that embankment. She didn't think Mercedes had it in her, and she'd proven her wrong, finally.

Yet that expression was the least of her thoughts. The way Syd held her, it'd felt so good. Those tight arms surrounding her, protecting her…she was meant for those arms. Mercedes almost gasped with that admission. Her? Meant for Sydney Campbell? Never! Right?

Holy fuck but she'd looked so damn lickable, her lean back flexing with every board she lifted. It should be against the law for a woman to have that many muscles. Sheesh! Mercedes rolled onto her side, groaning in pain when the fabric of the sheets brushed against her sunburned arms and shoulder. Worse, she was in her father's house. She couldn't even masturbate to relieve the sexual frustration of watching Syd's tight body all day.

Mercedes stared at the ceiling. Why hadn't she asked all the questions plaguing her today? Did the answers even matter anymore? The past seemed far away suddenly, almost irrelevant, yet the memories still had incredible power—those glorious nights spent getting to know herself and her sexuality, something she'd always known, no matter how many times she'd tried to deny it at first. Syd had known as well, and had proven it. They'd been so young, so full of explorations. Syd had made her face her insecurities, and heaven help her, Mercedes had loved every stroke of her calloused hands.

She slowly closed her eyes and gave in to the images. With Syd's gorgeous face on her mind, she let herself slide once more into sleep.

Chapter Eight

Guilt set in for Syd when Mercedes stumbled into the kitchen the next morning, her face and arms fire red, evidence of a sleepless night in the prominent dark rings under her eyes. She wore loose-fitting blue pajama bottoms and a gray T-shirt three sizes too big. Even in her frumpy attire, she looked good enough to eat, literally.

Watching her walk like a zombie across the linoleum, Syd felt like a total sap for taking her shirt back when she knew it was the only protection Mercedes had against the sun. She also knew her quick, angered decision didn't have anything to do with the ice cubes, or even the worms. It had everything to do with years long past them now, a hurt she'd sheltered for far too long. It was time to get over it. Certainly Mercedes had gone on with her life like their summer fling had never happened.

Syd had always thought herself above cruelty, and she was. But not with Mercedes, if yesterday's behavior was any indication. Mercedes brought out the worst in her, made her act like someone she wasn't. Guilt rubbed like salt against her raw conscience. What if she hadn't gone back to find Mercedes? Anything could have happened. Mercedes could have fallen deeper down that steep, rocky gulch. She could have spent the night there with broken bones.

"Hope *you* slept like a baby." Mercedes poured her coffee and dropped into a chair with a groan, not daring to put her back against the vinyl. Her glaring eyes looked up at Syd. "Thanks to you, I got to toss and turn all night with my flesh on fire."

"If you weren't so pigheaded, your skin wouldn't be fried." Syd dropped into the chair across the table from Mercedes as Miller strolled into the room.

"That's a nasty burn you got there." A smile dimpled the corner of his mouth as he regarded his daughter. "Forget to take a shirt yesterday?" He poured a cup of coffee and sat down at the head of the table with his morning paper.

Darlene bustled into the room already dressed for riding. Her eyes widened as she caught sight of Mercedes. "Holy cow. Have you totally forgotten all about ranch life?" She poked Mercedes's shoulder as she walked by.

"Ouch! What the hell did you do that for?" Mercedes glared at her.

"You should have worn a shirt."

"Jesus, would you guys shut up about the damn shirt!" Mercedes pushed away from the table.

"Noxzema will do the trick. And don't think you're getting out of our shopping spree today just because you are burned to a crisp and rescued cattle as well. I better watch out. You'll be after my job."

"Yeah, as if."

Miller looked up from his newspaper. "Syd told me what happened out there, darlin'."

"I damn near killed myself doing her job, if that's what you're talking about."

Syd glanced up, her behavior a little shocking after the lazy ride back to the house last night. For some reason, she thought Mercedes might still have some tenderness left in her. Guess she was wrong.

He chuckled. "Well, it doesn't surprise me in the least that you pulled off such a stunt all by yourself. I raised you, don't forget."

"And thank God for that. Otherwise, I couldn't have done a rancher's job all by my lonesome." Mercedes stretched her arms over her head and groaned. "I'm not going shopping, sis. Daddy, please tell her to stop with the stupid blue jeans."

Miller disappeared behind his paper, refusing to take any part in the argument.

"Oh hell yes, you are," Darlene huffed. "Either my boots get put to use on your skinny ass, or you walk outta here on your own. Ain't no sister of mine going street dancing in those la-di-da grubs you been wearing."

Before Mercedes could add another objection, Darlene grabbed her mug of coffee and, with a wink at Syd, headed out of the kitchen.

Syd couldn't help but grin. Darlene was one of a kind, not half as mouthy as her sister, but she could definitely hold her own.

"Good morning." Nelda's sweet voice came from the front of the house.

"In the kitchen, darlin'," Miller yelled out.

Mercedes rolled her eyes and tucked back a strand of hair that had escaped her band. "Great. More giggling, just what I need to go along with my headache."

"Aspirin," Miller said in a matter-of-fact tone.

Mercedes glanced over at him, then to Syd. "It'll be gone by Monday morning."

"Then stop complaining." Miller rustled the papers as he turned a page.

Nelda breezed into the kitchen, her eyes radiant as she pegged her sights on Miller. "Morning, gorgeous." She placed a kiss against his cheek and looked around the table. Her eyes settled on Mercedes with the same concern Syd had observed the previous evening. "How do you feel, sweetie?"

Mercedes opened her mouth to unleash the pits of hell, Syd was sure, but then she seemed to reconsider. "Just peachy, Nelda. Thank you for asking."

She arched her eyebrows at Syd as though in silent rebuke, and Syd realized she should have made the same inquiry. Instead, she'd been too busy looking at the way that Mercedes's shirt careened over those nipple rings, begging her mouth to stop watering.

Hastily, Nelda said, "I see things are back to normal around here."

"Things won't be normal around here until—" The clearing of her daddy's throat had Mercedes's mouth snapped back in place. She rose and added, "I'm going to take a shower."

Syd watched her leave the room, guilt and heat eating her alive.

When Darlene returned to the kitchen seconds later and slapped a jar of Noxzema on the table, Syd stared at her in confusion. "She might need help applying this. Thought you'd like the honors." She left with an evil grin.

Syd looked from Miller to Nelda, embarrassment crawling across her neck at Darlene's insinuation.

Miller shrugged. "Don't look at me. That growl has a bite."

Nelda grinned, but said nothing.

"You're both a big help." Syd pushed away from the

table. She guessed she was the only one who would take the challenge, and since she was partly to blame for the condition of Mercedes's delicious flesh, she knew she should step up.

With a final intake of breath, she left the Miller family at the table, all watching her as if in silent prayer for her safety.

Mercedes's door was partially open and when Syd rapped lightly, she heard, "Come in."

She pushed the door open and found Mercedes standing only three feet away, wearing nothing more than a lacey bra that did nothing to cover those nipple rings, and a pair of shorts. When their eyes met, thunder sounded in her mind. A softness traveled between them, like the barrier that had been there only minutes ago had suddenly vanished with the ascending of the steps. Desire flickered in those eyes, striking Syd like a lightning bolt. For several seconds, she could only stare, confused with the sudden change in Mercedes. Instead of leaving like her mind was screaming, she closed the door behind her.

"Let me put some of this on your back and shoulders. It'll take the pain away in no time flat."

The gentle expression faded and Mercedes's eyes narrowed into slivers of ice. "The only thing that will take my pain away is the plane that takes me out of this godforsaken place."

"Yeah, well, that, too. But in the meantime, I can do something about your flesh feeling like hot needles."

"A bit guilty, Syd?" Mercedes tucked that loose strand behind her ear and folded her arms just beneath her breasts, pushing her cleavage into an edible mound of red flesh.

"Maybe a little. The rest of the blame lies with you. You should try being nice more often. It gets different results."

"I wasn't the one who dumped water over your sleeping ass." Mercedes tapped her foot impatiently.

"I wasn't the one who decided to sleep in and welsh on a bet." Syd took a step toward her, her hands already shaking with the thought of sliding over Mercedes's curves.

Jesus, the woman had such power over her. Syd wasn't sure if she was pissed at herself for the weakness, or at Mercedes for knowing. Either way, the fact remained she was putty in the presence of this fireball. "Stop arguing and turn around. The quicker we get this over, the better."

Mercedes lifted that stubborn chin. "Just leave it. I'll take care of it myself."

Syd reached her in a flash, sick of the bitchy attitude. She grabbed her wrist and roughly spun her around. "Stop being such a bitch."

"Get your damn hands off me!" Mercedes tried to jerk away but Syd tightened her grip. "I will, as soon as you let me put this on." Syd tucked the lid of the jar under her arm and unscrewed the top. "Trust me, I don't wanna be touching you any longer than I have to." She dipped her fingers into the cream and spread it on Mercedes's back.

Mercedes cringed and arched her back. "Fuck, that's cold."

Syd ignored her and spread more Noxzema across the indention in her back. Mercedes sighed and gave in to the moment. With hesitation, Syd loosed her grip. When Mercedes didn't turn and punch her, she added her other hand to the heat of Mercedes's back. "There, doesn't that feel better?"

"Yes. Damn, that feels good." Mercedes moaned. The sound, like a locomotive, roared straight to Syd's pussy.

She stepped closer, working her hands delicately against Mercedes's heated flesh, inhaling the medicated sweetness of the cream, and Mercedes. God, she smelled so fucking good. Mercedes let her head fall back.

"Mmm. I remember those hands."

Syd wasn't sure Mercedes was aware of what she'd just said. Then she realized that her hands were no longer moving and that Mercedes was slowly turning around. The bitch was gone from those piercing eyes, and only a solemn woman remained. Mercedes licked her lips, not a sexual gesture, just a tiny lick on the edge of her dry lips. Syd followed the movement and lowered her head.

She half expected Mercedes to smack the piss out her. Actually, she wished she would. It would knock some sense back into the brain that was obviously short-circuiting. Hadn't she already been bitten once by this rattlesnake? Hadn't she fallen into the same trap before?

Yes, she had. But dang if she could stop herself from capturing Mercedes's lips against her own and pulling her body against her chest. She wove her tongue between those inviting lips and felt the release of Mercedes's sharp intake of breath, like a feather against her cheek.

God, I'm doing it again.

Mercedes moaned and Syd nearly came undone. Her knees went weak as she palmed Mercedes's ass, drawing her closer, grinding against her, and wanting to be deep inside her…to feel her come around her fingers just one more time. When Mercedes fisted a handful of hair, Syd released the guttural groan trapped in her chest and deepened the kiss, hungry and out of her mind with the need to fuck Mercedes harder than she'd ever been fucked in her entire life.

She lifted Mercedes's legs around her waist and walked to the bed, where she roughly fell on top of her.

Mercedes pumped against her, moving her hips in frantic circles. "Fuck me, Syd, please."

The words yanked Syd from her sexual trance. She'd heard those very words before, many years ago. Mercedes had begged to be fucked when she could take no more of Syd's teasing tongue and fingers. But before Syd could get near enough of her, before she could even begin to show her what their connection really meant, Mercedes was gone.

Syd hung her head, and ground her teeth in agony. "You're not doing this to me again."

She shoved off Mercedes and bolted through the door.

❖

"I'm not wearing those." Mercedes swiftly shook her head and darted for another rack, this one displaying thin slacks instead of those damn blue jeans Darlene was determined to foist onto her.

"Yes the hell you are." Darlene followed close behind, five pair of jeans hanging over her arms. "I'll not be caught dead with my sister wearing those ugly, plain things."

"Ugly...plain? My business attire isn't supposed to scream 'fuck me.'"

"Oh, trust me. It doesn't scream anything except 'tight, uppity, and stay the hell away from me 'cause I'm better than you.'"

Mercedes scoffed. "What the hell's that supposed to mean?"

"I just told you what that means." Darlene looked down the length of Mercedes. "How you going to get Syd to screw you again wearing this garb? Hell, anyone for that matter."

Shocked, Mercedes glanced around. The salesclerk was smiling at them, her pink lipstick and white eye shadow bright under the fluorescent lighting, obviously tuned in to their conversation. Mercedes grabbed Darlene's hand and led her away from the nosy bitch.

"First, I wouldn't fuck Sydney Campbell again if she were the last piece of pussy on earth," she lied, still shaken by the kiss and near fuck, and Syd's parting shot. "Second, my *attire* hasn't hindered my sex life in the least."

"Oh, those women you take home, screw, then shoo out the door before morning light? Yeah, I don't think they count."

"So what? I'm not looking for love. I'm looking for a fuck…and I get one whenever I want."

Darlene's mouth jerked into a smile, then she started giggling. "Oh shit, I think we just shocked ten years off the saleslady's life."

She curiously looked around and found the same clerk standing only ten feet away. "Do you mind? We're trying to have a conversation here. Don't you have some clothes to hang, or some advertisements to hang, or something?"

"Well, I never," the girl huffed. Tossing her white-blond hair over her shoulders, she stomped away.

"And your behavior shows, sweet cheeks. No one has fucked the bitch out of you yet," Darlene taunted, then laughed.

"What the fuck is so funny?"

Darlene finally straightened and swiped under her eye. "The poor salesgirl. You. Nelda. Everything since you got back here. And you, right now, thinking I'm too stupid to believe you wouldn't do Syd again if given the chance."

Mercedes yanked the jeans from her grasp. "You're full of shit. What in the world could that loser possibly have to offer me?"

"Um, the hottest sex you've ever had in your life?"

"Sweetie, trust me, Syd wasn't the hottest sex I've ever had. We were young, horny, and—" Mercedes clamped her mouth shut at the look on Darlene's face. She obviously didn't believe a word she was hearing. Even Mercedes could hear the quiver of the lie on her tongue. Syd had been the hottest sex she'd ever had. How many women had she been through to reach that conclusion? Dozens? Yes…and more. None had ever made her yearn with hunger the way Syd could, had.

When Darlene cocked her brow, Mercedes admitted caustically, "Fine, it was hot, and awesome." Totally busted, she let her chin fall to her chest and nodded. "It was the hottest sex I've *ever* had in my life. But that means nothing. She's stuck in this shithole town for life…wants to be."

Darlene let out a whoop of excitement. "I knew it!"

"You knew *what*?"

"You want her. You're already thinking about the future."

"No, I'm thinking about how fast I can get out of here." Mercedes darted through the display racks, past the glaring salesclerk, and into the fitting room. The mirrors on both walls showed her scarlet cheeks and heaving breasts. She looked flushed and her pussy slicked with remembrance of the kiss she'd shared with Syd only hours ago. What had it meant? Nothing? Something? Who could know? Syd had pulled away, even though she couldn't hide her desire. Why? She'd been on fire, the same fire that had engulfed Mercedes. Would they ever finish what they'd started?

She knew they wouldn't. Hell, she knew she couldn't. Syd loved her life out here in nowheresville, and Mercedes was neck-deep in her career. There could never be a future with each other, and she'd be damned if she did long-distance flings. She had more than enough pussy in LA…just enough to keep her hunger satiated.

She kicked out of her slacks and held a pair of jeans to her waist. The image looking back at her wasn't herself. Jeans weren't her thing, hadn't been since the day she boarded a plane and kissed this piss-pot town good-bye.

"You got them on? I wanna see." Darlene banged on

the fitting room door, snapping Mercedes out of her heated thoughts.

"This is useless, Darlene. I'm not fucking wearing those yeast-infecting jeans." She slipped her legs into the pants leg and buttoned them, curious if she could still pull off the look after her drought of never wearing denim. With curiosity, she spun around to see what she looked like from behind. Holy shit. The jeans lifted the cheeks of her ass up, holding them into a splendid mound. If she had to say so herself, her, in these jeans—well, there were possibilities, for sure.

"I found some shirts…belly shirts. Come on out. I wanna see!" Darlene tossed a shirt over the door.

Resigning herself to looking cheap and easy, Mercedes slid out of her blouse and pulled on the fraction of material. "Jesus. I might as well go naked."

She fastened the ties just beneath her breasts and eyed her reflection. What would Syd think about her with these low-cut, come fuck me jeans? Could she control herself? Did Mercedes want her to? Without a doubt, she knew she didn't.

She studied herself more closely. The jeans rested teasingly against the curve of her hips, her belly ring glimmered against the lights. Yeah, she could work with this.

She'd make Syd eat her fucking heart out, and then make her come all night long.

Chapter Nine

Syd leaned against the countertop and surveyed the crowd of locals and visitors gathered inside the bar. Beyond the fairgrounds, the streets of Loveland thronged with more people, most going to and from the amusement rides, while others gathered on the empty grass lot across the street to watch the live band test their equipment and amplifiers in preparation for the dancing later. Children squealed with delight as they bustled to and from the vendors with their cotton candy and caramel-covered apples.

The big Larimer County Fair and Rodeo didn't happen until August, but the smaller fairs always brought out the faces she hadn't seen for months. She normally got a thrill to be among old friends, but tonight was different. Tonight she wanted to be anywhere but here. She glanced casually around the room assessing the available women. Some she'd had, some not. Maybe she should go with her original plan and take one of them home for a night of sexual play. Would that erase the aftereffects of that heated kiss she'd shared with Mercedes earlier?

When someone called her name, Syd pulled out of her trance and tipped her hat to a woman with a tranquil smile. Heather had been a good fuck…not exactly electrifying, more pacifying and satisfying. Maybe Syd could cozy up with her for a little bit, convince her that a nightcap was in order. She was about to make her way across the room toward her when a woman she didn't know grabbed Heather's hand and led her onto the dance floor. Syd frowned and sank back onto the stool, all thoughts of a quick fuck ripped from her mind. Spending another night in the company of her vibrator wasn't what she wanted. Tonight she needed a warm body, caressing hands, and hours of hot sex.

Would Mercedes appear or was there way too much denim here for the uppity city girl she'd become? It was probably best if she stayed home and painted her nails, or pasted her face in that awful concoction she swore took off years of aging. She seemed to consider herself above such rustic gatherings, and her old friends didn't deserve the snub she'd no doubt give them.

With a sigh, Syd tilted the beer bottle to her lips and took a long, cooling swig. Even though she didn't expect to see Mercedes, she was still hunting for her face. Wishful thinking? Had to be. Her mind hadn't budged away from Mercedes since their mind-blowing kiss that morning. What had possessed her to lean in and capture those perky lips? Stupidity, plain and simple. No other reason she'd stick her hand in a rattlesnake nest.

Syd took another swallow of beer, determined to put herself out of her own misery and call it an early night. She'd just fall into bed fully dressed and pull the covers over her head. Only one more day and Mercedes would be gone, and things could get back to normal.

Alerted when a cowboy beside her sucked in a healthy breath of air and moaned in an undertone, Syd glanced sideways. His eyes were narrowed on something across the room and his expression was that of a hungry predator. Syd about choked on her own spit when she spotted spirals of honey-highlighted hair and glimpsed a face painted in earthy tones, black lashes feathering across her lids in a sensual caress. Only one woman she knew could carry off the model walk and tall posture at only five-feet-four. The air felt like it'd been sucked clean out of the room. Heads turned and the crowd parted as Mercedes strutted through with Darlene close on her heels.

As the last of the people stepped aside, she came to a halt a few feet from Syd, an image ripped right off the cover of a cowgirl magazine. Low-cut Levi's careened over her lean hips, set off with a black belt encrusted with silver rivets. A belly ring winked under the strobe lights, and the solid black halter knotted just beneath her breasts screamed "take me off." A pair of old black Gringo boots with silver chains dangling around the ankles completed the ensemble. And the lethal hip swing she was flaunting should've been against the law… it hypnotized grown men and caused them to act like randy adolescents.

Someone fucking kill me now. Syd squirmed against her stool as Mercedes talked to an old high school friend. Her smile was radiant, wide and genuine. What the hell had happened to her? Surely clothing couldn't transform a person. Could it? And where the hell could Syd find a duplicate of the fuckable woman in front of her, minus that poisonous tongue? This one had to be Mercedes's good twin, cause heaven knew her evil twin hadn't smiled since the second she roared to a stop in front of Travis Miller's house two days ago.

When Mercedes turned and draped Syd in her sea green stare, Syd knew she was a cooked goose. Before Mercedes boarded that plane to LA, she was going to be thrashing beneath Syd's weight. That was one promise little Ms. Rattlesnake could take back home to her perfect life. The only thing that could drag Syd's attention from the glorious creation in front of her was Darlene, who sauntered toward her wearing the biggest shit-eating grin Syd had ever seen on her face.

"Having a good time?" She eased onto the empty stool beside Syd and looked back at her sister. "Like my little transformation? Sexy, huh?"

Syd nodded and turned up her beer bottle, only to find out that she'd downed the contents already. She motioned for the bartender to bring her another and tried to look at everything else in the room besides that luscious example of sex appeal walking, talking, and laughing with old friends like they'd never parted. Men crowded around her, their smiles obvious as they tipped their cowboy hats, pushing at each other like high schoolers pining over their first piece of ass. Mercedes wasn't helping. Her radiant smile and batting eyelashes were enough to cause a fistfight. The poor saps had no clue that they were barking up the wrong tree. But Syd did. And before the night was through, she was going to lick the sap from that hard maple.

"Too bad her bite's deadly," she said, more to herself than Darlene.

"Since when did that ever stop you? If anyone can tame that tiger, it's you."

Syd met Darlene's knowing eyes. "Who said I wanted to tame anything?"

"You didn't have to. Darlene just knows these things."

Syd chuckled. "Does she now? Has it ever occurred to you that Darlene isn't always right?"

Darlene watched Mercedes with a sweet smile. "You're a great person, Syd. Go after what you want. I think you've waited long enough."

She slid off her stool and breezed away before Syd could question her. What, truly, did she want? It sure as hell wasn't Mercedes. Was it? As she watched Darlene push her way through the ever-growing crowd surrounding Mercedes, she wondered how she'd fallen for the wrong sister. Darlene was smart and funny and quick-witted, nothing like Mercedes. Of course, Darlene wasn't gay, though she had no qualms about those who were. Syd pondered the difference, mentally scratching her head as to how she'd fallen for someone like Mercedes to begin with. Damn, why hadn't she just turned and walked away, saved herself the mental turmoil? Did she just like inflicting herself with undue pain?

And then she saw Mercedes, climbing, scrambling, face masked in pain, making her way up that embankment. She'd shown courage and strength Syd didn't know she possessed. Had she not witnessed it with her own eyes, she'd never have believed Mercedes capable of such bravery. But she had, and watching her now, she wondered which Mercedes was the real Mercedes. Why was she constantly hiding that sweet, mature side of herself?

As she searched for the answer, she watched Darlene drag Mercedes into a line dance, three men hot on her heels. Their wishful thinking was engraved so plainly on their faces, Syd almost felt sorry for them. If any man believed he'd take the gorgeous woman home with him tonight, he was sorely mistaken.

Mercedes swung her hips, popping that splendid ass as she moved in rhythm with the music, perfectly matching her steps with the other dancers. All eyes were on her, watching every seductive move, ogling her—wanting to be with her, inside her, wrapped around her. How could Syd blame them? The same thoughts were buzzing in her mind like a swarm of bees in search of nectar, all exploring the many ways she could fuck Mercedes Miller before the stroke of midnight.

With the beer calming her frazzled nerves, she dragged her attention away from the undulating bodies and made her way outside. The fresh, cool night air did little to dampen down the embers. She found a nearby bench and planted herself on it, too afraid of her own emotions right now to watch another second of the show.

In the near distance, the ferris wheel circled, its occupants squealing with delight. To the right, a carousel of prancing horses emitted a rousing tune from its organ pipes as it whirled away. Vendors hawked their artery-clogging fair food while carnies called on people to take a chance and win a prize. The air was potent with funnel cakes, hot dogs, and fun. All around her, voices chattered and laughter rang out, almost mocking her loneliness.

Time passed while she begged herself to stop feeling...to stop wanting, to stop thinking. Before she knew it, the blocked-off streets were lined with people in chairs and blankets, families opening coolers to dole out juice boxes and cans of beer in anticipation of the live festivities.

She glanced around, already feeling the effects of the beer, past feeling the effects of Mercedes. What was it going to take to rattle the vixen from her mind? Fucking her? Watching that plane take her away from this town? When movement caught her eye, she turned and found Mercedes several feet behind her looking very uneasy sandwiched between two men, her gaze penetrating Syd like a laser beam. Though the men were trying hard to be perfect gentlemen, a green-eyed monster awoke in Syd. They wanted what she'd already had. And they wanted to be inside the woman she'd already been inside...and wanted to be inside this very second.

Syd quickly turned away from them, unable to focus through the cloud of images.

The band grouped together on the stage and the lead singer tapped her finger against the microphone. "Testing. Testing." She smiled at the crowd and waved. "Hiya, folks. I want to thank you all kindly for having us back again. We'd like to kick-start our night with a slow beach song. From the shouts and hoorahs coming from Jessie's bar, sounds like you all need a little cooling off."

The crowd laughed and then the guitar started, followed closely by the keyboards.

Someone tapped lightly on Syd's shoulder and she jumped and turned to stare up at Mercedes.

"Come dance with me so I can shake these cowboys, will you?"

Syd shook her head. "I don't dance."

"Scared?"

Syd smiled and leaned her elbows on her knees to support her already trembling body. "Nope. Just don't dance."

"Coward."

Syd nodded. "Yep, that's me." She let herself cruise Mercedes, taking a long look up and down that impressive body. "Besides, isn't putting yourself on display a little risky?"

Mercedes threw her head back and laughed. "Risky? For whom? Do you honestly think I give a shit what the hicks in this town think about me? After I leave, they can gab all they want. Makes no difference to me."

Syd studied her. She was lying. She hadn't expected Syd would call her bluff. She'd counted on her refusing the dance. If Syd took her up on the offer, Little Ms. Perfect would have to reveal who she was to the town she'd escaped from. Miller's daughter…*the lesbian*. Was she ashamed of the person she'd become, or the one she'd left behind?

With a smile of derision, Syd rose and tossed her empty beer bottle in the nearest trash can. "I've changed my mind about that dance. Lead the way, city girl."

Mercedes's eyebrows rose. She glanced around, taking in

the couples joined tightly in their slow sways. With a sigh, she downed the contents of her own beer and tossed it in the trash.

"How many of those have you had?" Syd asked.

Mercedes shrugged. "I'm not a cheap drunk, if that's what you're worried about...or hoping."

Syd wanted to remind her that she was dehydrated, and at this altitude, alcohol affected people more rapidly, especially if they didn't drink enough water. But this city slicker had forgotten a lot about her own upbringing and didn't appreciate being reminded of the fact. Syd decided to find a bottle of water after they danced.

Grabbing Mercedes's hand, she led her into the crowd. She was positive she heard one of the cowboys say, "No fucking way," but kept moving.

When Mercedes turned to face her, Syd knew the night was all but over. Soon, not soon enough, she was going to hear Mercedes moan once again.

CHAPTER TEN

Mercedes opened her eyes in an unfamiliar bedroom. She struggled to remember how or why she was in bed, obviously in someone else's house. Was she still sleeping? Hell no! Her head gave a burst of pain in answer to her question. She sat up and rubbed her thumping temples, staring around the room in disbelief. "Where the hell am I?"

When no one answered, and nothing stirred, she kicked the paisley sheets off and rose. Swaying on unsteady legs, she glanced down at a clock on the night table next to the bed. Four a.m. Sheesh, she couldn't remember the last time she'd risen before the alarm clock jerked her from sleep. Mercedes realized then what she was wearing. A man's white button-up shirt rested just below her waist, barely covering her ass. She struggled to remember how she came to be wearing it, but everything was blank.

The county fair. She'd been at the street carnival. Two cowboys were flirting like love-struck fools, and then… God. Mercedes looked down at herself again. Syd had been wearing that shirt and looked sexy as all get-out. Mercedes had wanted to take those clothes off her as their bodies swayed on the dance floor.

Jesus H. Christ, she'd danced in public with the object

of her infatuation, and it had been good. She hadn't cared that the town was watching, judging them, their prying eyes drilling into the two lesbians sealed to one another. She knew she should have cared—her father was a part of this town—but she couldn't. The woman on that dance floor, wearing jeans and halter top, with her emotions churning like a dust cloud, was her, through and through. And if anything, dancing with Syd was a tribute to how it all started, how her life had changed in a short time and made her the person she was today. She snickered at the thought. Those hot nights beneath the dark skies hadn't come close to making her the *bitch* she was today.

She wasn't entirely sure how that had happened, but it had, and she was ashamed of herself. Her family, Nelda included, didn't deserve to be treated with such disrespect…and neither did Syd. Mercedes jerked her gaze up toward the door, fear clawing through her gut. Had she fucked Sydney Campbell last night and blocked out every incredible moment? Please no. If there was anything she wanted to remember from this trip, it was having Syd make love to her again. She'd thought about nothing else since sharing that kiss. She'd wanted so much more.

She took a hesitant step toward the open bedroom door while memories flooded her mind. Beneath the moon, Syd's fingers plunging in and out, over and over, nursing her clit with gentle sweeps of her tongue while Mercedes screamed out her release. Had that happened last night? She focused on the chair beyond the door frame. She hadn't fucked Syd. Her body would know. She would still be sore from those splendid hands.

With a grateful sigh that she hadn't done the unthinkable and forgotten every flaming detail, she tiptoed to the living room. A handcrafted cedar coffee table was pushed away from a wraparound couch, where Syd was sprawled. In her sleep, she'd pushed the blanket aside, leaving her boxer-clad legs free for Mercedes mouth-watering view. Tanned, and lean as sin, her stomach and chest rose and fell, barely covered by a black sports bra.

Mercedes instinctively licked her lips, her head throbbing, and her pussy clenching. She took one last step, afraid to get too close, yet terrified not to. Syd's leg was bent, her arm slung over her face, and that damn dark tan beckoning Mercedes toward her. She wanted to crawl all over every inch of that tight body and do wonderful, unforgettable things with Syd... again. She could, she knew. A few more steps and she could be right where she left off all those years ago, right back to wild passion and insatiable sex. But where would that lead them? Where they'd started? Where they'd ended last time? Nowhere? Was it even a question she need bother with?

As she mentally licked those delectable legs and lean stomach, Mercedes knew Syd deserved better than anything she could offer. She had nothing to offer, as a matter of fact— just a sprawling city full of snarky people and a perfect condo in which Syd would look totally out of place. This town, this ranch, was Syd through and through. This was her home, her life, her past and her future, and Mercedes couldn't dream of taking that away from her.

She closed her eyes to shut out the sight. Aspirin and coffee would take away the throb in her head. If only it were as simple to find an antidote for the ache between her legs.

❖

Syd watched Mercedes pad around the kitchen, her slender legs teasing from beneath the hem of the shirt. She'd been cute as hell when Syd escorted her into the house hours earlier, trying with all her might to be the gentleman her mother raised while Mercedes pawed at her. How badly she'd wanted to fuck her, to just splay her out across the bed and drive herself deep inside her. But she couldn't take advantage of a dehydrated, drunken woman. Guess that was another thing Mercedes had forgotten about her.

Now watching her, Syd wanted desperately to stroll into the room, lift her onto the counter, and make a breakfast out of her.

Her mind screamed for her to get up and her body demanded she obey. Juices slicked her pussy as Mercedes reached for something above her head, lifting the edge of the shirt to reveal the same silky pink panties Syd had wanted to remove when she got her home. How was it possible for a woman so sexy to have a tongue as sharp as a razor? And why couldn't Syd summon the willpower to resist her? With an animalistic growl, she pushed off the couch and went after her prey. God help her, she was going to fuck this woman for the rest of the day, and to hell with the consequences. She could beat common sense back into her head after Mercedes flew out of her life once again. But for now, her body needed something more, and Mercedes was going to quench that thirst.

When Mercedes turned to look at her, Syd almost lost herself in the gut-wrenching need filling those eyes. In her hand, she held out a mug, almost like an offering—as if that should, or could, stop Syd. Her eyes widened when Syd closed the gap to within a single foot and fixed a smoldering gaze on her. Her hand shook as she pushed the mug toward Syd. "Didn't know how you liked it."

Bemused, Syd could only stare at those penetrating eyes while her pussy throbbed with yearning. "Yes, you do. I like it hot. And sweet." She took the mug, placed it on the counter, then pulled Mercedes into her arms and crushed their mouths together.

Wild, needy, and clinging to each other, they stumbled toward the bedroom and fell across the bed, grasping at one another. Syd kicked out of her boxers, then moved her attention back to the edible mound lying before her. Mercedes let out a sharp cry when Syd ripped the shirt open and drew on that pierced nipple like it was a bottle made for only her mouth. She'd thought of nothing else from the second Mercedes had let her bathing suit top crumple around her narrow waist two days ago. Syd flipped the metal against her teeth while she drew the hardened nipple between her lips, pulling, sucking, tasting, and needing. Her body thumped with the most unbearable want for this woman, for this long-overdue fuck.

Mercedes mewed like a kitten and panted, "God, yes! It's like a path of fire straight to my pussy. It's fucking incredible."

Syd sucked harder, swirling her tongue over metal and hardened flesh. Mercedes tugged at her hair, clawed at her back, and arched into a bow. She moaned and cried out, squirming against Syd.

"Get inside me, Syd. Please!"

Needing no further invitation, Syd kneed her legs open, pushed the edge of her panties to the side, and drilled her middle fingers deep inside.

Mercedes clutched at her, screaming out her pleasure, and then her body poised into a stiff line. "I'm com…I'm fucking coming, Sydney."

Syd pumped her fingers faster, deeper, harder, while Mercedes bucked beneath her like a stallion fighting for freedom. Syd held her down and thrust against her G-spot, submerging her fingers with every pump. Mercedes's insides squeezed and spasmed, gripping Syd's fingers like a vise. Syd ground her teeth against sweet pain when Mercedes raked her nails down her spine. She plunged deeper, deeper still, filling her completely.

Only when Mercedes slumped against the mattress in a worn-out heap did Syd withdraw. Waves of disappointment swept through her. She'd waited so long to hear those cries of passion, and now it was over almost before it'd begun. She kissed Mercedes's throat, and nibbled her way up her neck to suck her earlobe.

"God. That was, amazing." Mercedes slowly wound her fingers back into Syd's hair, tugging her closer. "And how the hell did I get here? I swear, I only had three beers…that I can remember."

Syd hovered above her, lost in the moment, in those breathtaking eyes. How? How in the world could she allow herself to do this again? Wasn't she wise to Mercedes's tactics this time? Of course she was. She was a grown woman. But this time, she'd ensure Mercedes would carry a lot more memories away with her, adult memories, not those of inexperienced teenagers' exploration.

Syd ground her hips against Mercedes, arching tightly. "Dehydration and way too much sun, remember?"

Mercedes's expression went from content to needy. She leaned forward and captured Syd's lips, slicking her tongue inside her mouth, and then thrust her hips forward. She rolled Syd onto her back and mounted her, grinding her pussy against her pelvic bone. "We've come a long way, you and I."

Syd wasn't sure what she meant, but the way she was arching that back and rolling those hips, who cared? She palmed Mercedes's hips and drove herself hard against her. Jesus, she was going to come just watching that undulating body, all of her memories now in flesh form for her taking. Mercedes's thick mane of hair tumbled over her shoulders, making Syd want to grab it like reins while she fucked her from behind. The dirty, nasty, delicious thoughts rushing through her mind were painful.

Mercedes's lips parted as she ground faster, pumping her pussy more desperately against Syd's body. Syd could barely stand the sound, yet couldn't move while Mercedes used her like a personal vibrator. Nor did she care. This was how she wanted Mercedes, vulnerable and unstoppable, like the woman she dreamt of. This was what she wanted to remember when Mercedes left her once again.

"Tell me, Syd, did you ever think about me? Want me?" Mercedes panted, practically thrashing against Syd's body.

Syd didn't know how to answer. She hadn't expected anything personal to be shared between them…just wild, clingy sex, and lots of it. To avoid going near what her mind wanted to scream, she draped her hand behind Mercedes's neck and pulled her down.

"Kiss me while you come again." She parted Mercedes's lips with the tip of her tongue, and inhaled her pheromones.

Mercedes moaned, grinding in lazy circles, and then her body tightened. She slung her head back and screamed out her release in a long, sharp cry, rocking wildly.

Syd clung to her, on the verge of coming just watching Mercedes thrash like a wildcat, and then Mercedes fell limp on top of her, sucking in healthy, gulping breaths of air. When she half-consciously kneed Syd's legs apart, Syd came undone. She grabbed Mercedes's hand and shoved it between her legs. "Make me come, Mercedes."

Mercedes leaned up, a smile stretching those delectable lips, and then shimmied down her body, kissing, licking, and slithering her way down until she was settled between her thighs.

"I remember what you like." Mercedes swiped her tongue against Syd's clit.

Syd responsively jerked against the sinfully wet torture and lifted her hips for more. Mercedes ran her fingers along the slit of her pussy, teasing with the tip just inside her opening, then licked her clit once again.

"Oh, God, just like that." Syd closed her eyes and wove her fingers into Mercedes's hair, pulling her closer, recklessly needing relief. "Quit teasing me. Make me come."

She heard the desperation in her own voice, knew it would only prompt Mercedes to do just that, to tease her into a tight ball of yearning woman. When Mercedes pressed two fingers inside and sucked her clit, Syd came on contact, her body jerking with the rhythm of her pumping orgasm. God, it was tearing her apart, racking through her in exquisite waves of pleasure. She hadn't felt those powerful spasms since…since Mercedes.

Mercedes drilled her fingers in and out, rough, then gentle, just the way Syd liked it, just the way she needed it. She'd taught Mercedes how to please her, showed her how much she liked having Mercedes please her. And Mercedes had remembered.

Why?

How?

When her arms went limp beside Mercedes's head, she knew Mercedes wouldn't be the only one leaving with memories. Syd would be left with a host of her own to haunt her days and nights.

God, what had they done?

Chapter Eleven

Mercedes awoke with a start, Syd's body spooned in a web of arms and legs around her. Morning sunrays filtered through the curtains, giving a soft glow to the room. The world was tranquil, humble, and…heavens above, that naked body was so warm and cozy, and fit perfectly against her curves, like matching pieces in a puzzle.

She glanced at the clock on the nightstand and gasped. "Holy fuck. I gotta go!"

Syd grabbed at her just as she hopped out of bed. "What for? We don't have to help set up for the wedding. Someone was hired to do that." She leaned over and glanced at the clock. "Wedding's not for another five hours. Bring that sexy ass back to bed, why don't ya?"

Mercedes found her jeans beneath a heap of clothes and tugged them on. The wedding was actually happening and she felt small-minded that she'd ever planned to disrupt it. Her daddy was happy, and she could see that now. Nelda might have outwitted her, had a comeback for every sarcastic phrase Mercedes could throw at her, but when Mercedes needed her most, she'd been there with gentle hands and soft murmurs.

With her heart warming as she thought about the hours ahead of her, Mercedes picked up the barely there shirt she'd worn to the fair the night before and wrinkled her nose. "I can't wear this again." Finally looking at Syd, she swallowed a lump of desire suddenly rising in her throat. "Got one I can borrow until I get back to the house for something decent? I don't know what I was thinking tromping around in public in this tarty thing."

Syd sat up on the edge of the bed. "What are you wearing to the wedding? Don't you and Darlene have special dresses?"

Mercedes blinked. "Not that I know of." She looked away from that glorious body, knowing one more of Syd's warm glances would have her back in that bed and she'd never get home. And no way was she making a fool of herself wearing some country hick bridesmaid outfit to the wedding. She had to get home and make sure she had a better alternative if her sister had lost her mind and ordered some lacy, cheesy dress. "I have to go. Darlene must be on drugs if she thinks I'm going to go to that wedding—"

Syd was beside her before Mercedes could complete her sentence. She grabbed Mercedes's arms and harshly spun her around. "Darlene told me what you came back here for—to sabotage their wedding. And I'm warning you, don't do anything to ruin the day for them."

Mercedes caught her breath at the roughness of those hands, that tousled hair, those piercing eyes screaming to be heard. She pulled out of Syd's grasp with a glare, her chest heaving, not in anger, but in lust. What was wrong with her? She was acting like she'd never seen a just-fucked woman before. Not a single one of the dates she'd slept with had ever looked as edible as Syd did right now. Mercedes met that glare with one of her own, upset that Syd thought so badly of her she was already jumping to conclusions. Mercedes supposed she couldn't blame anyone for suspecting her motives—she'd made her attitude pretty clear. But it still hurt that Syd gave her no credit and hadn't noticed the thaw between her and Nelda. The look on her face made Mercedes want to shrink back.

"I'm not—" she began, but Syd wasn't listening.

"Are you that self-centered that you'd destroy everything that makes that man happy?"

Mercedes narrowed her eyes. "Self-centered? You're calling me self-centered while you live off my family?" Fury bubbled like a witch's brew, exchanging lust for hatred in milliseconds. "Why don't you go find a real job and stop living off your dead dreams for a change? My daddy only took you in because he felt sorry for you, because you were pitiful, and homeless."

A sarcastic smile edged Syd's lips. "That shows how much you don't know about your own father. You could only dream of being half the person he is." Not a bit intimidated by Mercedes's death glare, she added. "Why don't you take your uppity ass back to the big city? You don't belong here, you never did."

Stung by her words, Mercedes said, "This is my home, Syd, like it or not. You have no right to lecture me about my father's happiness."

"Someone has to, because it doesn't seem like you give a shit." Syd stomped to the dresser. "How do you think he feels when you never come back here? This place is his life."

"Well, it sure as hell ain't mine. I've made an honest living for myself, and I'll be damned if you make me feel bad about my success." As soon as the words escaped, Mercedes felt their bite—felt how untrue they were. Sure, she'd climbed those ladders, and she'd reached her goals, but for what? Most of the time she was miserable. That's not what she'd dreamed her life to be. Yet she lived it daily, all while thinking about the one woman who stirred her life in ways no one ever could.

With a jerk, Syd tossed a T-shirt at her. "Here, wear this.

At least you'll look human while you behave like an alien to your family."

"Listen to who's talking," Mercedes flared back. "The woman who hasn't spoken to her own brother in years!"

Fire sparked in Syd's eyes as she fisted her hands by her side. "How dare you bring that piece-of-shit loser into this conversation. As you well know, I had no control of the things he did. You, however, can make choices." She took a step closer, those fists still curling and uncurling by those sturdy thighs. "Why don't you go pack your shit and fly on back to your precious city lights? This town's already seen enough of your poison."

Mercedes gasped. "How dare you!" She took two steps toward the bedroom door and quickly turned back, confused why she couldn't get her mind settled long enough to have the perfect comeback. The conversation was already too far out of control, and she'd heard just about all she wanted to hear out of Syd. She stammered like a fool, shifting from foot-to-foot, tears threatening. "Go to hell, Sydney Campbell!"

"Trust me, darling, I'm in it right now. And, remember, no one in this family will allow your vicious games to tear those two apart, starting with me." She glared for good measure.

Mercedes bit back her instinctive response. Syd had everything all wrong, and from the look on her face, she wasn't going to be easily persuaded to believe Mercedes had changed her mind about this wedding. However, Mercedes knew she hadn't helped with her lashing tongue, either. At this rate they would never stop quarrelling long enough to communicate on another level. She searched Syd's face for a glimpse of the tenderness she'd seen the day before, and again this morning. How could she recapture those moments riding home with Syd's arms around her, when they seemed to belong together?

Did Syd have the same feeling, or did she only see Mercedes as a fuck?

Mercedes was afraid, but she was determined to be honest with Syd. For once. She drew in a long breath, desperate to cease this argument. This wasn't the way she wanted to finish her day, especially after the perfect way it'd began, lying in Syd's arms. "Syd, listen to me. I'm not pretending I was happy about the wedding, but you're right. I haven't been the most perfect daughter, but I'm here now and I want—"

"I know what you want," Syd cut across her scornfully. "You want to mess up everyone's lives, then walk away without facing the consequences. That's your MO, Mercedes. That's who you are."

Syd's caustic condemnation stirred something in Mercedes's gut. Sick to her stomach, she shrugged into the shirt and grabbed her boots from by the door. "That's who you want me to be. It's easier for you, isn't it, if I'm the one who lets people down, not you?" Slamming her feet into the boots, she reminded herself what she was really doing here, and it wasn't to find happiness in Syd's arms. "We should have left our memories beneath that oak tree. They were better off there, dead and buried."

Shutting her mind to the hurt in Syd's eyes, Mercedes turned and stormed from the house, hating the vengeful lie she'd just allowed to roll from her mouth. Those memories were far from dead. Hell, they'd done nothing but claw through her mind year after year, day after day, minute after minute. She ran across the dry grass and didn't slow down until she was sucking in healthy gulps of much needed air. Acrid tears stung her lids and she roughly swiped them away, too angry to let that woman make her cry. An image of her mother fluttered through her mind and she let out a sob. No one could take her place, but Nelda wasn't trying to. Mercedes didn't know why she hadn't seen that immediately. Nelda was just being herself. She'd made a nice home for everyone. Didn't she have a right to put her own touches there? The place wasn't a mausoleum.

Chatter caught Mercedes's attention as she approached the backyard. She passed the fenced-in pool and drew in a deep breath when she saw the transformation. Men and women moved around each other, constructing a large gazebo. Tiny white lights twined around green ivy, encasing the white columns. The creation was artfully woven between carefully draped panels of white gossamer silk, shot with silver. White roses studded the structure, giving it the look of a fairy bower awaiting its lovers. Mercedes stared in awed amazement at the beauty coming to life right in front of her. It was like watching an edition of *Bride* come to life.

Mercedes was suddenly overcome with doubt once more. Maybe Nelda's kindness was just a show. The woman knew she had to win Mercedes over and she'd been working it since the moment they'd met. Mercedes bit her lip, confused. She knew she shouldn't be won over by the elegance in front of her, or by a few motherly gestures. What if Nelda wasn't as innocent as she seemed? What if she was the con artist Mercedes had suspected from the start? Mercedes had to know.

Filled with determination, she went inside and found caterers bustling in the kitchen removing finger foods from numerous large Styrofoam containers. Her mouth watered at the aromas, reminding her she was long overdue for food. She could hear her father's voice coming from the living room and headed in his direction. Heat burned her cheeks. How was she going to handle this? Tact wasn't her strong suit.

Mercedes slowed her steps and waited for her father to stop talking to the caterer. As the man walked away, her daddy turned around and greeted her with a twinkle that made her panic for a few seconds. Jesus, did he know where she'd been all night, what she'd been doing all day? Did it show on her face?

She marched up to him. "We have to talk about this wedding."

He gently wrapped his large hand around her arm and guided her further away from the kitchen. "What's on your mind?"

Mercedes folded her arms across her chest and lifted her chin. "I'm not sure if she's right for you."

A fire lit up in his eyes, a fire she'd never seen. "You've been on hell's path to shut Nelda out from the second you walked through those doors. You're out of line, honey. Nothing, and no one, is going to stop this wedding. Do I make myself clear?"

"Daddy, please. Listen, I—"

"You don't get to decide my fate, Mercedes." He ushered her toward the den, a room only used by special guests. "You don't know anything about Nelda, nor have you given her a chance. She's not the evil witch you claim her to be, and you've treated her with disrespect."

"I most certainly have not. She—" Mercedes yelped as he turned the knob and pushed her through the open door.

"Why don't you take a look around before you say another word, Mercedes. My patience has worn thin with your childish, arrogant behavior." He flicked a hand toward the room.

Mercedes caught her breath. There, beneath the bay windows, rested a shrine to her mother. Two large curio cabinets lined both sides, packed adoringly with her mother's figurines and trinkets with soft light illuminating every shelf, and the walls were cramped with her and Darlene's school drawings, some she'd only seen in the box her mother kept in her closet. More picture frames dominated the walls across from the window, all snapshots of their younger days. Every frame held a picture of their mother, most with her hugging and smiling down on her daughters with love and pride.

She moved to the window, tears streaming down her face, her mind overflowing with unanswered questions.

"She did this?" Mercedes fingered the large ceramic angel in the center of the round table. A wreath of red carnations, the very one that had adorned her casket, lay preserved in a circle as if guarding the smiling angel. Mercedes felt her heart stumble.

"Yes. She'd have no part of removing your mother from this house. As a matter of fact, she refused to move in here initially. She said this was your and Darlene's home, where your memories would always be." His eyes were narrowed, but soft. "Listening to you, I think she may be right about that. So I've been looking at a place on the other side of Fort Collins."

Mercedes whirled around to face him. "You're moving?" Suddenly, the thought of losing her father outweighed the worries about his remarrying. "No! You can't move."

"We'll talk about that later. Right now, it doesn't matter. What matters is that you get this harebrained idea of stopping this wedding out of that pretty little head of yours."

"I don't want to stop the wedding," Mercedes said quietly. "All I wanted to know was that she's as good as you think she is."

He strolled toward her, his face bearing the lines of age. He was still so handsome, with laugh lines creasing the edge of his eyes. Her mother, his children, and his family, had given him those features...not Nelda. Yet the face Mercedes was used to from their annual vacations together had changed. Her father had lost the disheartened expression Mercedes had seen too often. When his face relaxed he looked...happy.

"I'm lucky to have her," he said. "I've made mistakes in life and God has seen fit to give me some happiness all the same. I'll take it where I can find it, thank you very much."

Mercedes let her gaze linger over the mementos of her mother. She felt like the biggest spoiled brat in the world, and foolish about her doubts. Her daddy was no fool. He'd never have allowed a fraud into the house. Nelda was awesome and she was going to add a few more laugh lines to her daddy's hard face, Mercedes was positive of it. With a smile, she wrapped her arms around his neck. "If she hurts you, I'm unleashing the devil."

He squeezed her and laughed, the sound like magic against her ears. "You haven't already?"

She withdrew and pursed her lips. "Nowhere even close."

Chapter Twelve

Mercedes stared down at the maroon dress Darlene handed her. Her first instinct was to curl her nose in distaste. Maroon? Whatever was her sister thinking? Mercedes wouldn't look good in that disgusting color. And were those pearls sewn into the cuff? No way was she wearing this.

When she looked back up, she found Darlene staring at her, awaiting her response. "Well?" She gave a tiny bounce, but Mercedes knew she was ready to bust open with a joker smile.

Damn it, she couldn't let her sister down. Hadn't she done that enough over the past years? "It's amazing, Darlene," she said, cramming her voice with sincerity before she choked. "I love it."

Darlene released a squeal and threw her arms around Mercedes's neck. "Thank heavens. I just knew you were going to hate it."

Mercedes squeezed her back, wishing she could take them both back in time, to when they were closer than any two sisters could be. She suddenly wanted to race across the pasture on the horses, wanted to skinny-dip in the lake and stay up all night and chat about nothing special at all. Was there a way to make up for the past years, possibly rebuild the void she'd placed between them? She wanted that so badly.

"Try it on, I wanna see." Darlene dropped back on the bed and curled her legs under her.

Mercedes did as instructed, biting back the groans as the satin slid along her skin. She normally wouldn't be caught dead in a dress like this. But today wasn't her day...today was her family's. Once the dress was in place, she turned so Darlene could pull the zipper up. The sound alone was like nails on a chalkboard. The feeling made her feel ashamed all over again. Man, she'd surely turned into a high-class twat, and until this very moment, she'd never truly seen it.

She twirled for Darlene, who smiled and bounced on the bed before she rolled onto her back, her smile slowly fading as she continued watching Mercedes. "I guess you're going back tomorrow."

"Yes, I have to. There's a big trial coming up."

"It must feel good doing what you do—you know, having people count on you to solve a crime." Darlene's face was serious. "You help them get justice. That's amazing. I could never do your job."

Mercedes was shocked. It was the first time Darlene had said a word about her career. Hell, she wasn't sure Darlene even knew what she did for a living as all she ever called it was "that high-falutin' job."

The words touched a part of Mercedes she didn't realize was still alive. "Yes, you could. As a matter of fact, with the way you argue everyone down, you'd make a fantastic lawyer."

Darlene twisted her nose. "Lawyers are nothing more than con artists in designer suits."

Mercedes busted out laughing and hopped on the bed to lie beside her. "You got that right. You'd shit if you knew how much a lawyer gets an hour for their damn secretaries to type a paragraph and mail it. It's ridiculous."

Darlene rolled onto her side and propped on her elbow.

"How'd you know you wanted to be a crime scene investigator, or whatever the hell you are."

Mercedes didn't correct her, she was just thrilled that Darlene had gotten that close. She shrugged. "I knew I wanted to help someone, somewhere, though I knew I didn't want the medical field. Scalpels and guts make me hurl."

Darlene giggled, but her eyes stayed focused on Mercedes. For the first time in her life, Mercedes saw Darlene looking up to her, hanging on her every word. It was breathtaking. The apple of her daddy's eyes could never do wrong, and yet, here she was looking up to the one person who'd abandoned her.

What a shit she was for ripping herself from their lives, Mercedes thought. How could she make it up to the both of them? Could she at all? When Darlene looked down, Mercedes caught something else in her gaze…something sad. "Is everything okay?" she asked.

Darlene hesitated. "There's something I want to talk to you about. Later. After all this."

"We can talk now," Mercedes prompted. "No time like the present." She wondered what Darlene had to say that was making her act so out of character.

"No, I said I'd help Daddy." Darlene twisted a wad of hair around her fingers and her eyes darkened with doubt again.

Mercedes recognized the gesture from their childhood. Whenever Darlene had done something wrong, she fidgeted with her hair the same way. "What's it about?" she pressed her.

"It's nothing." Darlene rolled off the bed and escaped out the door like she wished she'd never said a word.

Mercedes followed her down the hallway to their father's room. He called them in after they'd knocked. He was almost ready, wearing an elegant black tuxedo over a starched white button-down shirt. The getup made him appear ten years younger. Mercedes stood back and watched as Darlene adjusted his tie. He looked so handsome, years younger than she'd seen him looking in a long while. She smiled as he fidgeted and pulled the knot at his throat.

"Darlene, you're cutting off my air supply."

"Sorry, Daddy, but you keep pulling it down." Darlene smacked at his hands as he reached to loosen the tie once again. "Stop it!"

Just watching the two of them sent a pang of longing through Mercedes. She missed them so much, missed their closeness. Feeling completely ashamed for abandoning everyone the way she had for the sake of her career, she blinked back hot-stinging tears. Who was she kidding? Her career hadn't done this, she had. She was to blame here, and she knew it. Didn't they say 'hell hath no fury like a woman scorned'? She'd allowed bitterness to fester like a sore until it took over and ruled her entire life. Worse, she'd treated her family like trash to avoid returning to this ranch. She couldn't change the past, but today of all days, she knew the future was being shaped. She had some important choices to make.

"Nelda could care less if my tie is perfect or not," her father said.

"Well, *I* care. I don't want my daddy meeting his new bride with his tie all crooked. What will your friends think when they see a scruffy groom?"

He dismissed her fussing with a laugh. "They'll think how pretty Nelda looks in her gown. No one will notice I'm present."

Mercedes angled her head at his sweet words. He was in love, once again. How dare she attempt to fuck that up for him. She should be ashamed for treating Nelda the way she had, how hostile she'd been, and how nasty she'd acted. She already knew she had not been completely honest about her motives; in fact, she wasn't exactly sure why she felt so strongly. But seeing the shrine created in her mother's honor had helped her put things into perspective. She couldn't freeze time. Nelda's gesture was incredibly sweet, and it meant the world to Mercedes. It also made her realize that she'd never created a memorial of her own. She had never really let go, and it was time she did.

Mercedes sighed. Nelda was good to her daddy, and perfect for him, and instead of finding everything wrong, she should have opened her eyes to the love they shared. A love she didn't have. Not that she'd truly ever wanted to stand under a bower like the one in the backyard and pledge herself to another person. Her life was great, wasn't it? Money, friends, and all the fucks she could possibly want. Who needed love?

As organ music drifted through the open second-floor window, Darlene squealed, "Oh, my God. It's time! We have to get you downstairs." She ushered their father out the door and into the hallway.

Mercedes followed them down to the kitchen, her heart dragging. She needed love. She did, and she knew it, and she wanted it, somehow. Would she ever find it? God, her father wore it so well...shining brightly in his eyes. Love wielded one helluva punch, and it glowed all around him. Could she wear it with just as much appreciation for what the simple, fragile word held?

She grabbed his arm just as he turned to start out the door, his family and friends all turned to wait. "Daddy, I love you."

He grinned and pulled her close. "Not half as much as I love you." He gave her a squeeze and held her at arm's length. "Your mother would be so proud of you."

Tears welled and fell over the brink. Those words were lies, and if anyone knew it, her father did. Her mother had wanted her strong-willed and independent, but she would have been shocked that Mercedes had traded her heart and her soul, all for the sake of a career that often made her miserable and only added to her cynicism.

How could she help but be cynical? Nightmares plagued her dreams on a normal basis after she'd processed crime scenes. People were so cruel to one another, killed without so much as a care or an afterthought. Heartless criminals roamed this earth, and her job was to prove their guilt. But, truly, what help was that? She could only bring closure to a case—and by that time it was too late to save the victim. That's what saddened her the most, the inability to heal the pain of the loved ones left behind. And now she'd stabbed Syd with her vicious words. Something else she needed to make amends for before she left this ranch. Her future might very well depend on her turnabout.

Her father wiped one of her tears away with the pad of his thumb. "No tears today, baby, only happy faces."

Mercedes nodded and he headed out the door. Within minutes, he'd be a married man again…to a woman with whom he shared a tremendous love and who made him sparkle with life.

Darlene faced Mercedes, her maroon dress tailored to her body. She looked so pretty with baby's breath twisted into her French braid…a mirror image of their mother. She hugged Mercedes. Tears rolled down her cheeks. "We're smearing our make-up!"

Mercedes laughed and pulled out of the embrace, sniffling and dotting her eyes with the tip of her fingers, careful not to smear her matching dress. "I've been such a bitch."

"Yeah, well, we're all used to it." Darlene chuckled as more tears fell down her cheeks.

Mercedes straightened, waved her hands across her face in an attempt to dry her tears, and let out a cleansing breath.

"Come on. We have a daddy to give away. Let's get this show on the road."

❖

Syd fastened the pearl necklace around Nelda's neck, then hooked the matching bracelet around her wrist.

Nelda fingered the pearls and stared at her reflection in the large antique floor mirror. "Wow, I never thought I'd be getting married again. Actually, I swore I wouldn't."

"Why's that?" Syd indicated her reflection. "You make a beautiful bride."

Nelda swatted her arm. "Child, you say the sweetest things." She sat down on a lounging chair and patted the one opposite. "Sit, let's chat for a minute."

Syd did as instructed, a little nervous. It wasn't like Nelda to ask her to sit before they talked. Normally they rattled on about anything under the weather without any formality. "Is something wrong?"

"Lord, no, child. I'm about to marry a great, great man. Life couldn't be any better." Her eyes sparkled as she gave Syd one of her famous sweet smiles. "Travis and I have been talking about our future…about the ranch, and his retirement."

"Yes, he's mentioned that possibility."

"What do you think about it?" Nelda fingered the lace trim around her waist.

Syd was taken back by the question. "Me? I don't know. I mean, I knew one day he'd hand over the reins to Darlene…" She trailed off, feeling a little sappy about what else she wanted to add. "I can't imagine him anywhere else but the ranch."

Nelda reached out and gave a sympathetic pat to her hand. "You adore him, it shows. And he's got a strong liking for you as well."

Syd nodded and looked away. Were those tears she felt threatening? She couldn't remember crying, not ever…not when her parents died, not when she had her dreams ripped out from under her feet, and surely not when her brother trotted out of her life. But she'd been very close, the day Mercedes broke her heart. There! She'd admitted it, if only to herself. Somehow, losing Mercedes had topped everything else she'd ever lost.

As if Nelda sensed her discomfort, she prodded on. "I was just wondering what your plans are. Are you planning on staying on at the ranch? Travis has told me you have a dream of running your own place some day."

Syd nodded. But suddenly, that dream was no longer as strong as it had been the day she vowed to achieve that goal. For some reason, running the ranch outside this family made Syd sad, made her long for something she hadn't lost yet. "I've been here for so many years. You guys are my family now. As long as Miller and Darlene want me to stay, that's what I'd like to do."

Nelda leaned forward and poked her knee. "And that's exactly what I told Travis you'd want to do. So, after the honeymoon, he'd like to sit down with you. He's thinking you might want to add some more land to your holding. And bigger responsibilities."

Syd widened her eyes. She couldn't believe what she was hearing. Was Miller thinking about making her a partner in the D&M Cattle Company?

❖

Mercedes followed Darlene down the aisle after their father. A long red carpet led their way to the gazebo. At the end, standing proudly by her daddy's side, was Sydney, looking way too delicious to be the "best man" wearing a matching tuxedo and a smile to melt the moon right out of orbit.

Would she allow Mercedes to apologize? Who could blame her if she told her to go fuck herself? Mercedes made a mental note to find her after the wedding, after the newlyweds had scurried off to whatever night they had in store, and ask her to listen to everything she had to say. It was time to get things off her chest, once and for all.

Syd gave her a watchful look, no doubt waiting for her wrath to open up and rain down over all of them. Dear God, how she'd missed those sexy eyes, and longed for so many years just to know what Syd looked like now…what she'd feel like. She'd been lying to herself way too long.

And here they were, yet again, back where they started, beneath that oak tree, only now exploring the years in between, the women they'd become. Right now, with Syd's eyes twinkling with lust and a hint of anger, Mercedes knew Syd was the better woman. She'd held rooted to her dreams, and her beliefs. She was strong, and genuine. Mercedes had changed after her breakout, freedom ringing high with her much-needed departure. The woman she'd become was not the woman her mother wanted her to be.

The fact was unnerving.

Too late to back down now. Her career was tucked tight under her belt and her life was driving forward on its own accord…just like she'd planned it all those years ago. Sure, it was without romance, or companionship, but that was okay, right? Wasn't it?

As she dragged her gaze away from Syd's sexy features, she knew there wasn't room enough in her life to admit love into the equation. But without a doubt, if there were to ever be love, Syd would be the one. Hell, she probably always had been.

If only their paths hadn't taken them in different directions, if only Syd had called her. She shook the thoughts from her mind. There couldn't be any what-ifs. There was no room for them, and that was that. With any luck, she'd get to enjoy her final day here on the ranch in the company of those pleasing hands before she headed back to normal life...with her head held high.

She plastered a smile on her face and continued down the aisle. Today, Nelda was going to make her father a happy man...everything the greatest man she knew deserved.

❖

Syd shifted from one foot to the other, not nervous about being in front of the entire congregation, but to be in the presence of Mercedes after fucking her all morning...and after the words they'd thrown in anger.

She wasn't sure what had changed Mercedes's mind, but the evidence of tears made Syd let down her guard a bit. Was it possible this wedding could go off without a hitch?

An image of Mercedes, naked, lips parted as Syd tore an orgasm from her body, flitted through her mind. God, it'd been incredible, even more appetizing than she would have guessed. And now that beautiful woman was walking down the aisle toward her, looking sexier than she'd ever seen her, smile bright, eyes glassy from tears. Those tears showed heart, showed compassion, and it was astounding to see. Of course, she knew that, deep down, Mercedes did have a heart under that cool "I don't care about anyone else" exterior, but seeing her softer side was an entirely different matter. It was breathtaking.

Another image fluttered through her mind. She caught her breath as it rooted. Mercedes, white dress flowing around her legs, hair down and billowing in the breeze…walking toward Sydney…the groom. Jesus Christ, her heart jumped to even think of such far-fetched things. Mercedes would make a gorgeous bride. Without a shadow of a doubt, Syd knew she'd never want another like she wanted Mercedes right now. Who was she kidding? She'd always wanted her, possibly had from the second she first saw her on that truck.

But what could she do about it? Mercedes wasn't catchable. She adored her life of high-class condos, designer clothes, and chaotic courtroom dramas. She didn't have space for Syd inside her world. Furthermore, she didn't want her there. And who could blame her? She had the life she'd always wanted, a good salary, and an endless supply of women to use for her sexual gratification. A monster awoke inside Syd as she envisioned Mercedes in the arms of another woman. No doubt, she'd fuck 'em and leave 'em slick with satisfaction. The thought was unbearable.

Mercedes stepped onto the platform and turned to face the entrance, but not before giving Syd a shy smile. Syd's insides melted at the gesture. Somehow, she knew this wedding was going to be perfect…though her own life was far from it. She gave a slight nod, then diverted her gaze away, unable to watch her right now, worried she might give away the emotions churning like a raging bull in her stomach.

When Miller turned and gave her a wink, Syd could almost see the humor behind his eyes, as if he knew being this close to his daughter was tearing her apart. No, not being this close—being so far away. Always so fucking far away. Sweet Jesus, she loved this woman, and there wasn't a damn thing she could do about it. How was she going to part with Mercedes when the time came for her to leave? This time, Syd knew, she might never get over it.

The wedding song began, and Nelda started down the aisle

in a simple off-white gown shaped to her form. She looked radiant as she kept her eyes focused on her handsome groom, her bouquet held tight in her grasp.

If only Syd could have that. It was amazing to see how love brought such joy, even more agonizing to live in its presence every day of her life—yet be without it.

When Nelda stopped beside Miller, she slowly turned to look at Mercedes. Syd held her breath, awaiting the raging storm. Heaven knew she didn't want to drag off a kicking screaming spoiled brat, but she would to make sure this wedding carried on.

A loving smile lit Mercedes's face, and a single tear slipped down her cheek. She mouthed the words, "Thank you."

Nelda hugged her tightly. The moment was the most precious thing Syd had ever seen. She choked back tears and watched as Nelda placed the bouquet in Mercedes's hands. The congregation *awwed* and sniffles could be heard from several women in the front rows.

Syd felt frozen in time, and before she knew it, the wedding was over. People crowded around the newlyweds as they followed them toward the front yard, tossing bird seed and rose petals. Chatter and laughter mingled as Syd tried to focus and to stop thinking. When she spotted Mercedes silhouetted against the sky, waving at the departing car draped in toilet paper and whipped cream, she headed her way. The reception and barbecue weren't until this evening, and she planned to have Mercedes again before then. Again, and again, and again.

Maybe slaking her constant thirst for this woman would help when it was time to say good-bye. And this time, there would be a good-bye. Even if it took the last breath in her lungs to say the words, she'd be damned if she let Mercedes leave this town without hearing her.

Chapter Thirteen

Syd hadn't said a word since she escorted Mercedes to her pickup after the ceremony. She didn't have to, Mercedes could see the lust written all over her face. Her gut churned like a bend in a rushing river as she quietly followed Syd onto the porch and through the front door of the cabin, unsure what to say, unsure of anything except the wild need tearing through her body.

When she turned to look at Syd, to tell her she was sorry for the words she'd spat in anger, to say anything to break the silence invading her mind, Syd was there, towering over her like a barbarian she-god, that delicious dark tan illuminating those chocolate eyes.

Mercedes felt like a fairy princess beneath her height and her mind stumbled for the words she longed to say. "Syd, I need to—"

Syd put her finger against Mercedes lips, silencing her. "Shh. Don't say anything. Don't."

She leaned down and replaced her finger with her lips. As if Mercedes was nothing more than a wisp of smoke, Syd bent and scooped her into her arms. Without a break in stride, she carried Mercedes to the bedroom and laid her across the bed like a delicate porcelain doll. Mercedes wanted to rip at her tux and shed her own binding dress from her body, desperately wanting to feel their flesh slick and firm as they moved against each other. But those slow hands gliding down her ribs and over her hips stopped her from rushing the moment.

Syd settled between her legs, and a hand crept under the hem of her dress, stroking the inside of her thighs. Mercedes caught her breath as those fingers gripped at her, pressing her legs apart, torching her from the inside out.

"Syd, please…"

Syd leaned forward and hovered over her, not touching, just eating her alive with that sexy gaze. After what felt like eternity, she lowered herself onto Mercedes, slowly pressing her hips against her enflamed pussy. She captured Mercedes's lips in a passionate kiss, memorizing her mouth with that exploring tongue.

Too many emotions rushed through Mercedes's head as she wove her fingers around Syd's neck and held on tight, pressing upward to meet each thrust. Faster, harder, faster still, she ground their bodies together with her ankles locked behind Syd's back. Her lips were still sealed against Syd's when her orgasm burst through her like a kaleidoscope of sensation. She moaned into Syd's mouth, gripping her neck, holding Syd tightly against her quivering body.

Syd moved up and with a hand on either side of Mercedes's head, she watched as Mercedes convulsed into spasms. Grinding against Mercedes's throbbing pussy, she commanded, "Look at me."

Mercedes opened her eyes and met a gaze so raw and open that it jolted her to the core. The truth pumped through her mind as hard as the orgasm rocked her body. *I'm in love with Sydney Campbell.*

And then Syd was falling over the edge with her. Head thrown back, she groaned, rocking against Mercedes in wild, frantic movements, arms quivering as she held herself upright.

Then she fell over Mercedes and they lay in silence, their bodies trembling as one.

❖

Sydney slowly eased out of bed, away from the heat of Mercedes's naked flesh, and walked to the bedroom window. She couldn't think anymore, her brain felt like mush. Hell, she'd done nothing but think while she held Mercedes close to her. She'd lost count of the times they'd made love during the few hours they'd stolen before the events planned for later that day. By now people would be noticing their absence. And by now she should be sated. But their time together wasn't nearly enough, and the ache in her gut was only getting stronger, more unbearable, with every second that ticked away.

The digital clock on her dresser glowed like an unwelcome beacon, reminding her that time was running out ferociously fast. Come morning light tomorrow, Mercedes would be gone, probably for good this time. Syd pulled the edge of the curtain back to see the sun setting and movement in the distance, people coming and going from the Millers', preparing the big barbecue bash in honor of the newlyweds.

She didn't want to go, didn't want to move from this house or waste a single second of precious time while she had Mercedes in her bed. What the hell was she going to do? Plead with her to stay? Ask her to make room in her life for a damn country hick? What a laugh that was. Syd would only muff her perfect world. Besides, didn't she have her own life to live?

She turned away from the window to gaze at the beauty curled on her side in the bed. With her honey-streaked hair feathered across the pillow and her dark lashes fanned across her cheeks, she looked like an angel. Admittedly the angel could be a sharp-tongued, foul-mouthed, sexy witch, but Syd didn't care. It was all she could do to resist the urge to climb back in bed and fuck her once again.

Mercedes shifted and hugged the pillow to her. God, she was beautiful. *Mine.*

Syd smiled at the thought, at her wishful thinking. In truth, Mercedes wasn't hers and never could be, and the sooner she accepted that fact and tucked their encounters away in the darkest recesses of her mind, the better off she'd be. Maybe one day, just maybe, she'd find someone to make these images fade, to make the yearning go away. Of course, not a single woman had come close to making them shimmer, let alone erasing them, but there was still a lot of life left in her. It could happen.

Just not with Mercedes.

Mercedes stretched and opened her eyes. A smile lifted her lips as she caught Syd watching her. She patted the bed. "Come here, sexy. I know we have to go back, but I'm not done with you."

❖

Mercedes padded to the kitchen in one of Syd's button-up shirts, her body aching in all the right places, her pussy splendidly sore from making love. She couldn't remember ever feeling so overly comfortable. She wasn't even this comfy in her own condo. There she barely ever walked around in anything less than designer pajama sets. Being in this house, wearing nothing more than a thin shirt, was like…home. She could truly get used to this freedom.

She knew Syd's shirt was going to wind up in her luggage for the trip back to LA tomorrow. Damn, leaving was only a blink away. The days had vanished before she could come to terms with all that had happened. She was going home in the morning so she could be ready for work on Monday. All she had was the rest of the day and night to spend with Syd and her family. The thought made her stomach coil into a tight knot.

She was going to miss them all. More amazingly, she was going to miss the ranch. Was it possible to get homesick for a place she detested? No, no it wasn't. The Edwards trial was coming up, and the prospect of nerve-wracking court appearances weighed on her.

The case was complex and the DA was looking for the death penalty, so the burden of proof was very high. She knew the guy was guilty, and normally she thrived on the challenge of working with key forensic evidence. She always thought about the victims and wanted to see justice done. But this time she felt uneasy. Edwards had slipped through the net before, and the police were desperate to get him behind bars. Everyone involved with the forensic evidence was under incredible pressure, and Mercedes thought that must be why she felt so reluctant to go back. But LA was her life and she loved that life, right?

As she poured coffee into her mug, Mercedes heard the jets from the shower. She pictured a delicious, tight, sexy body stepping beneath the pelting spray, a body she'd enjoyed all night long. Syd had made her come more times than she could count, and it shocked her that her body flamed to life just from thinking about those hands, that mouth, everything she'd done with both.

A quiver ran down the length of her and her stomach rolled. Maybe she could spare some time to visit the ranch? Maybe a weekend, or even two, each month? Was that too much to ask? Too much to hope for? Would it be fair to ask Sydney to commit to a long-distance relationship?

Mercedes blinked hard. *A relationship?* This wasn't a relationship. This was pure sex, a weekend filled with fucking and catching up on old times, with nothing personal between them. She'd deliberately avoided asking about the past, or why Syd hadn't called after Mercedes left for college. It didn't matter anymore. The questions that had burned in her soul for so long were unimportant. Syd's reasons were her own. The choices she'd made had hurt Mercedes, but the time had passed for explanations. Mercedes couldn't care less about the reasons right now.

She made her way into the bathroom and slipped out of her shirt. The silhouette of Syd behind the glass doors made her mouth water and her libido crash into overdrive. Today was her last day with that tight body and those magical hands. And tonight would be her last night. She knew she'd spend it with Syd, and tomorrow, when she left for home, she'd leave Syd behind. Next time they saw each other maybe they wouldn't want to tear off their clothes. Maybe she wasn't really in love and this infatuation would just burn itself out. In the meantime, Mercedes couldn't fight it. Naked, and out of her mind with need, she eased into the shower behind Sydney.

When Syd started to turn to her, Mercedes pressed her hard against the cold tile and molded herself to her back. "Anyone told you how fucking sexy this back is?" She knelt and licked the indention of Syd's spine.

"Yeah, quite a few people, as a matter of fact. My back is like a legend around here, didn't you know that?" Syd chuckled playfully and arched as Mercedes continued her explorations.

"Really, now?" Mercedes curved her tongue across one splendid mound of cheek, this time taking a sharp nip against that athletic ass. A monster had awakened, something she wasn't used to feeling. Fuck if that wasn't a pang of jealousy crawling through her. She shook her head against the immaturity and kicked Syd's legs wider. "Well, they're right. It's tight, lean, totally lickable, and so damn sexy."

"Glad you approve. But it's not my back aching right now." Syd circled her hips to emphasize her need.

"Ah." Mercedes slid a single finger into her wet depths and pumped twice. "Is it this spot?"

"God, yes. There." Syd's head fell back.

Mercedes grinned, her own pussy flaring to life. "Are you sure? It couldn't be here?" She slid her fingertip through the folds and traced a circle around Syd's clit.

Syd's hips jerked at the touch. "Fuck, yeah. Right there."

"Anyone ever tell you that you have a potty mouth? Keep it up and I might be forced to put something in it."

Syd laid her face against the tiles, a hand flat on either side of her body. "Promise?"

Mercedes drilled two fingers up inside her.

Syd moaned. "I don't know if I can handle this again."

Mercedes pressed her lips against Syd's cheek. "Oh, but you can, Syd. I remember your body could take a lot more than what I've given it over the past two days."

She almost jolted back from her words. Hearing them roll from her mouth was like a slap in the face. Everything they could have been, they were not. All they had was this moment, the few fleeting hours they could steal between their broken past and a barren future. The thought saddened her. Was she missing this in her life? This need, with someone quenching her thirst, and filling her heart?

And this ranch. Where once she couldn't stand the thought of coming back, for some ungodly reason, she dreaded the fact she was leaving so soon. How could that be? Nothing had changed here. Nothing at all. Wasn't ranch life everything she'd wanted to flee from? And Sydney? Hadn't she wanted to stay as far from her as possible, too? How in the hell had she gotten herself right back into the same predicament she'd been in all those years ago?

God, it was going to be so fucking hard to say good-bye this time. And this time, she couldn't just write it in a letter. She'd have to see Syd on her way out that door. She'd have to tell her good-bye face-to-face before she flew away, once again, and this time Mercedes knew what she was leaving behind.

The thought made her stop and think. For a crazy moment she was tempted to stay. But she couldn't throw everything away. She'd worked her tail off to climb the career ladder faster than most of her colleagues. She had a great future ahead of her, if she wanted to spend the rest of her life reconstructing horrific crimes.

Evidence doesn't lie. The words echoed in her mind and she reached around, down Syd's stomach, through her thick bush, and spread her lips with two fingers. What was the evidence telling her now? What did Syd want from her? And what was she willing to give?

Mercedes increased her pressure, and Syd hissed and let out a deep, throaty groan. "Make me come, Mercedes."

Mercedes pumped harder, faster, circling her fingertip against Syd's clit until it hardened into a beaded mound. Then Syd was coming, her whole body trembling, her hands balling into fists, and her sharp cries echoed around the confines of the shower. Once more Mercedes was falling over the edge of a precipice with her, once more abandoning herself to the private world she shared with Syd, only ever with Syd.

Chapter Fourteen

Syd carried her plate of hash to a picnic table covered with a snowy white linen tablecloth, set it down beside Mercedes, and then slipped onto the bench beside her. They'd spent the late afternoon making love again until they couldn't hide away any longer, and the wicked high she got just being in Mercedes's presence still surprised her. A wink, a smile, even something as small as a flip of hair over her shoulder sent Syd's nerves barreling to the edge. And those new jeans and sexy shirt she was wearing drove sparks of lust through her body. A glimpse of that tight ass or bare midriff made her weak. The only thing keeping her from carrying Mercedes off to a secluded room in the ranch house was the presence of Travis Miller.

Normally, during family gatherings, Syd sat with Darlene, but Seth Potter had been by her side from the second Mercedes and Sydney arrived, no doubt avoiding Miller at all cost. Syd kept a watchful eye on Miller, amused that he hadn't tossed the punk kid turned man out on his ears, by his balls. She was even more amused that Darlene had found the balls to invite him. Miller detested Seth's no-good father, and the dislike was well deserved.

It was cute to watch the new couple giggle like teenagers.

Lust kept them locked in each other's sights, and the possibility of love sparkled all around them. Syd ached for the same thing, something she was almost positive she'd never have. And to make matters worse, no one had batted an eye when she and Mercedes had finally arrived—together. She'd expected stares, knowing smiles, Darlene's witty comments. But there'd been no reaction. Everyone behaved as though the absence of Mercedes from her father's house in the lull after the wedding ceremony was natural. It was as if the whole family knew what Mercedes and Syd were fighting so hard to hide and had accepted it.

Mercedes scooped up a forkful of hash and chewed absentmindedly. "Yummy. I haven't eaten hash in…too many years to count." She took another large forkful. "Except for my never-ending love for Mountain Dew, I'm normally a health nut. I wonder if the caterers have a Web site I could order from. I might seriously have to stock up on some of this before I leave."

Syd looked away. Mercedes's casual words left more of a sting than she dared admit. She glanced down at her half-empty plate, her appetite draining. How was Mercedes able to carry on such a normal conversation, as if everything they'd shared over the weekend stood for nothing, just a hot few hours easily forgotten…another cog in the wheel of life?

Syd wanted to shake her, tell her there was more, that there'd always been more. And if they wanted to, they could open themselves to all kinds of possibilities. Why couldn't they at least talk about it? Syd wanted to have that conversation, but Mercedes's flippant chatter was sending a signal that *she* didn't. Struggling, Syd contained herself. God, this parting was going to hurt so much. The loss was so much deeper than her first departure. Much as the knowledge cut like a knife, she wouldn't change a minute of their time together…not a single moan, taste, or sweet caress. She could never regret a second exploring Mercedes's exquisite body.

When Darlene tapped her finger against the microphone, Syd looked up and tried to concentrate. Darlene stood in front of the gazebo, all smiles, her eyes mischievous and happy. Seth stood to the side, waiting patiently, his nerves showing as he fidgeted from boot to boot.

"If I can have everyone's attention, it's time to toast the bride and groom." Darlene looked directly at Syd, then at Mercedes. "Sis, can you bring your city butt up here?"

Mercedes groaned, a flush crawling up her neck and across her cheeks as she rose. "I'm so going to fucking kill her."

She made her way through the maze of tables and chairs, the crowd clapping, until she was standing beside Darlene. Syd's heart stumbled at her beauty. Mercedes wouldn't admit it, possibly didn't even know it, but she'd changed in the short amount of time since her arrival three days earlier. She looked more relaxed and she'd let go of her slick, superior city attitude.

A smile found its way to her lips at the thought that she'd contributed to the change. Only a few days earlier Mercedes was an uptight woman hell-bent on clobbering any hope of this wedding taking place. She'd been on the outside of her family and this community, and seemed to like it that way. Now Syd was not so sure about that, and the thought gave her hope. She was nuts to be optimistic, and maybe she was in denial, but she couldn't believe Mercedes would leave tomorrow and never come back.

"I'll go first since, by the look on Mercedes's face, I'm going to be a dead woman shortly." Darlene turned to Mercedes and rolled her bottom lip out in a pout. "I wuf you."

Mercedes laughed and Syd knew there wasn't another woman for her. The one who held her heart captive was unavailable, was the most breathtaking creature she'd ever known, and she was leaving with the sunrise, taking Syd's every breath with her.

Darlene faced Miller and Nelda, her wine glass held high in front of her. "Here's to many years of married life, and all the wrinkles growing old together brings with them. I love you both." She toasted and people *awwed* and laughed at the same time.

Syd smiled. God, how she loved this family, and this ranch, and being a part of both. Too bad Mercedes's heart wasn't rooted to home. She'd give anything just to see her face every day, even with her snarky attitude and foul tongue. Syd was sure this ranch could change her heart if she'd just give it a chance…if only she'd open her mind to the beauty around her.

Darlene handed the microphone to Mercedes and a hush of anticipation rolled over everyone. These people might not have seen the wild child in many years, but her reputation for spunk would never die. Half of them probably expected her to say something patronizing, or worse, something unkind. Syd knew otherwise and was surprised by her certainty about that. Her view of Mercedes had altered. Was that what love did? Was she just blinded by her emotions or was she looking at the real Mercedes at last?

Mercedes hung her head for a brief second, then she looked toward Miller, the tears brimming up in her eyes making them sparkle like diamonds. "There's not another man on earth who could sit on the same pedestal with my daddy. I'm lucky to have him, and he's the luckiest man in the world to have found Nelda." Her gaze moved to Nelda. "You've made him a happy man again, and you belong together." She raised her glass in a toast. "Thank you, Nelda, for putting that smile back on my daddy's face, and for the Scrabble game."

Mercedes winked at the newlyweds, and Syd lost her sanity in a hail of conflicting emotions. She all but held her breath as Miller and Nelda rushed to the girls for a warm embrace. When Syd looked around, paper napkins dotted most of the women's faces while the men stared in silence at the special moment.

And a special moment it was. Mercedes showing heart, what a rarity that was, and now it'd been shown two days in a row. Syd knew she'd never forget this singular day, or that beautiful face. Mercedes's barriers were down and her heart was on her sleeve for everyone to see. God, she was magnificent.

An hour later, Syd crept through the crowd and found a secluded spot against the side of the gazebo, where she lingered to watch the children play. She wasn't sure where Mercedes had disappeared to, and it was just as well. All she'd done was gaze at her ever since they left her house earlier. Syd's emotions were in turmoil, the what-ifs vying for answers. Was it fair to ask for more? Could she? Should she? Her heart screamed yes, but her mind told her she would be asking for more than Mercedes could ever give. She longed to tell Mercedes how she really felt, that she loved her. Would she be shunned, or ridiculed? Was it a risk she was willing to take?

She glanced around in hopes of finding that gorgeous face, hoping the answer to the rest of her life would be resting in those eyes. When she didn't find what she desperately wanted to find, she turned back to the kids and smiled as a little girl squealed. She'd been tagged and started tapping the heads of the other children as she started around the circle.

Travis Miller cleared his throat. "I thought you might need a cold one." He held a beer bottle out and Syd happily took it, wondering how many six-packs it would take to dull the coming blow.

She knew she could easily drink herself into a stupor, anything to stop the railway of memories she was sure would invade her mind very soon...when the ranch was quiet once more, and the scent of Mercedes no longer lingered on her pillow. With a sigh, she pushed the thought away. No need to dwell on things she had no control over. Mercedes was a person she couldn't control—well, besides when she was breathlessly coming. Syd ground her teeth hard and looked away.

"Nelda and I have changed our plans a bit." Miller turned up his beer and studied her. "We're so excited to get on with the honeymoon, and some vacation time, we found an earlier flight. Leaves late tonight."

"Can't say as I blame you wanting to get away," Syd said. "What time do you need a lift to the airport?"

"Darlene's offered to take us, and from the looks of them..." He tipped his head toward the cozy couple. "I'd say he might be coming along for the ride."

Syd turned a quizzical eye on Miller. "You spared his life, that's a start."

Miller shrugged. "She thinks I hate him. Figured as long as she thought that, I'd keep my little girl safe from his clutches." He smiled. "He's a good enough fella, though his daddy can eat the cow dung off my boots. Surely can't spite a man for his daddy's wrongdoings, now can I?"

Familiar laughter caught Syd's attention long before the sight of Mercedes did. Her smile was wide and genuine as she and Darlene laughed at something Seth had obviously said. Mercedes looked like she didn't have a care in the world, like she wasn't leaving Syd in less than twenty-four hours, like leaving was going to be the easiest thing in the world.

Syd sank deeper into a trough of self-pity. It pulled at her heart to watch how relaxed and happy Mercedes seemed. They'd only just gotten to know one another again, and now she was leaving and that didn't seem to bother her one bit. Syd knew she should have swallowed her pride and gone after Mercedes a long time ago. They'd wasted so much time. If only Mercedes would stay just a little longer, long enough to want to stay forever. If only Syd didn't love her quite so much, she might survive her leaving.

"If you need any help with the ranch, Fred said to give him a shout," Miller told her.

Syd dragged her sights away from the woman who was about to discard her like a pair of jeans that tugged too hard at the crotch. "Don't worry about the ranch. Everything will run smooth as glass."

"I'm not worried a bit. If there's one thing I don't ever stress about, it's this ranch. It's never been in better hands." He clapped Syd on the back. "There are some things I'd like to go over with you when I get back from Jamaica. Nothing pressing, just some minor changes I'd like to make."

The conversation with Nelda waded through her mind. "No problem. Just enjoy your honeymoon, and don't let that receding hairline get sunburned."

He chuckled. "I plan on having the time of my life."

Syd found her gaze traveling back to Mercedes. She almost gasped out loud when she caught Mercedes staring back. Syd couldn't wait to take her home tonight, to make love to her every second until the very last moment when she was forced to say good-bye...until Mercedes had no choice but to say those words too. Maybe she wouldn't. Maybe good-bye would feel just as hard for her as it did for Syd. She could hope.

"If you don't mind my saying so," Miller shifted to move slightly in front of her, still watching his daughters with pride, "your daddy was a fool for not believing in you."

Something stirred in Syd's chest. She hadn't talked about her father in a long while. It was better off that way. Each time she thought about what he'd ripped from her, handing over the ranch her no-good brother never deserved, it made her angry all over again. However, there was some comfort to hear those words coming from a man she admired, and whose opinion she respected. Miller's words were as good as any paycheck he could offer her.

She slowly nodded. "Yes, sir, he was. He knew my brother was worthless. He also knew the ranch was all I ever wanted. I'll never understand why he did it. I can well assume his old-fashioned rules about women and their roles in life blinded him. Doesn't make it right, though."

"I'm sorry for your loss," Miller said. "Although it led you here. I couldn't be happier with your work, and the love and devotion you give to this ranch."

"Thank you. That means a lot."

"But you should be careful." A smile tugged his lips as Darlene high-fived Mercedes. "I hear foolishness is hereditary. Unlike your father, you should always trust your heart and go after what makes you happy. It would be a shame to have you lose something very precious twice in your life."

He clapped her on the back once again and moved away, leaving Syd confused, yet not at all confused. She knew what he was talking about. And she knew exactly what she wanted, but the woman she desperately needed was out of her reach. So fucking far out of her grasp it was like having no hands at all.

CHAPTER FIFTEEN

Mercedes resisted reaching for Syd's hand as they strolled down the path through the woods behind the ranch house. The sun had sunk behind the trees, outlining the tall pines in silhouette and filtering between the branches of the oaks. Saying good-bye to her daddy had been hard, yet exciting. He was starting a new chapter in his life and Nelda was going to take very good care of him. Of that, Mercedes was now sure. They'd hugged and sniffled, giving each other knowing smiles, and she and Syd had stood side by side to watch them drive away.

With a snicker and crimson brushing her cheeks, Darlene had made it clear that no one should wait up for her, smiling like a demented fool while she snuggled against Seth. Thankfully Seth had finally stopped his fidgeting long enough to relax around her daddy. That was a big thing to Travis Miller. He'd have no part of anyone who stuck themselves into a corner, uncomfortable with mingling. Seth had proven himself worthy of their father's approving eye. And even though his daddy had done an awful thing, Mercedes could see that Seth wasn't going to let the past affect a possible relationship with the Millers.

Watching Darlene shift her weight next to him, Mercedes

ached for that "foolish" love. It was sweet to see her sister so love-struck, though also scary. For some reason Mercedes had always pictured her single for life. It boggled her mind to think of Darlene married, kids clinging to her legs screaming for Mommy. Yet Mercedes could see her being a good mom one day, like theirs.

"Your speech was very sweet." Syd finally broke the ice between them. She kicked a stick out of the way with her booted foot.

"Thank you." Mercedes looked up at her but Syd's eyes were trained on the path before them. She looked way too damn delicious in those Levi's that were loose in some spots, perfectly tight in others. Yet Mercedes had wanted nothing more than to remove them all evening. Fantasies of Syd instantly supplanted the domestic daydreams of Darlene. Mercedes wanted Syd naked against her body, and that was just for starters. "Guess I managed to stop being a bitch long enough to see she really was good for Daddy, huh?"

As soon as she said the words, she felt resistance, as if a wall had grown or a door had been slammed between them. Syd had something on her mind, her quietness proving that fact. Mercedes was afraid of whatever it was, fearing it would spoil their last hours together. She peeled the leaves from the twig she'd picked up from the ground, anything to keep her hands busy. They were alone and the tension was high, lust even higher as they made their way toward their beginning... toward that damn oak tree.

"Does that mean you'll be visiting more often?" Syd asked after a few minutes. "More than once every thirteen years?"

"I'm not sure if I can get back again anytime soon," Mercedes said. She wondered what it would be like to become a more frequent visitor. Would she arrive one day and find a woman living in Syd's home? The possibility made her jealous and her voice sounded thin when she spoke. "The next five months are always the most chaotic at work."

"Your daddy enjoyed having you back." A branch brushed Syd's legs. She kept it from whipping back and hitting Mercedes. The gesture screamed "Syd"...always the gentleman.

"We're going on vacation at the end of the year, to Florida," Mercedes said, hearing the note of defensiveness in her voice. "Looks like it won't be just the three of us this time."

"I'm sure Travis is looking forward to it. But it's not the same thing as having you come back...home."

Mercedes hung her head, hating the direction the conversation was leading. "This hasn't been my home in many years."

"This is always home...home never goes away."

They rounded the bend where the trail narrowed and the branches hung low. Moonlight broke through the canopy of trees, illuminating their special clearing. Mercedes's heart raced in anticipation. Only a few more yards to the beginning... to the breathless nights learning about herself in Syd's arms. As the woods closed around them, so did the darkness. Light wasn't needed here, never was. She could have found her way back here blindfolded.

"Syd," she said softly, almost sadly. "You know as well as I do, I was never good at being a rancher's daughter."

"That's not true. Just because you rebelled against ranching doesn't mean you couldn't have found a life here. There's more to Colorado than working your daddy's ranch."

"Like what?" Mercedes wanted to retract the question as soon as it met her own ears. Actually, she wanted to avoid the entire conversation. It was obvious where it was headed...to a place she couldn't face just yet. "I hated everything about living here." When she looked ahead, she saw the tree she knew so well standing gracefully against the narrow pines. "Well, almost everything."

A smile lifted Syd's lips, though in the darkness it was hard to see if the humor touched her eyes. "Brings back memories, huh?"

Mercedes nodded and looked down. Syd's arm dangled between them. All she had to do was reach out and take those fingers, entwine them with her own, and the moment would be perfect. The two of them, together, hand in hand, enjoying a peaceful stroll on her land…their land—Mercedes couldn't deny that everything around her was as much Syd's as it was hers.

"You never answered my question about coming back here more often." Syd pushed a branch aside and waited while Mercedes moved ahead of her.

To say yes would lead Syd to believe there could be more between them. To say no would be a lie. Mercedes did want more. She stopped in front of the tree, staring up at the branches reaching high into the sky. "Man, this bitch is huge. I don't remember it being so massive."

Syd moved in behind her, enclosing Mercedes's waist in her strong grasp. "Talk to me, Mercedes, and not about this damn tree. About this weekend, next month, next year. *Us*."

Mercedes sighed. The moment of truth was upon her. Syd wasn't going to let this die. How could she tell Syd that although she loved her, it didn't count? There wasn't room in her life for sentiment, or for flying to and from the ranch for weekend fucks? Things couldn't work that way. She slowly turned and hardened her heart in the same motion. Syd was amazing, incredible, to be exact, and she deserved so much more than Mercedes had to give her. "I don't make promises I can't keep."

Syd locked her hands at the small of Mercedes's back. "I'm not asking for promises. I'm asking..." She moved forward and touched her lips to Mercedes's cheek. "Could there be something more?"

Mercedes wrapped her arms around Syd's neck. "We have tonight. Let's make the most of it." Hot tears stung her lids. "Anything more...I think we need to be realistic, Syd. Long-distance flings just don't work."

"What if it wasn't a fling?"

"What are you saying?"

Syd didn't answer at first. She was still choking down the hurt cramping her chest. Mercedes hadn't lied to her, hadn't made promises she couldn't keep. Syd couldn't ask for more than that. They were two adults and Mercedes was being honest. She saw Syd as a fling, not a potential partner. As much as she wanted to rush home, to curl into a ball and cry in self-pity, Syd had this one last night and she was going to use every minute wisely. That didn't include pressuring Mercedes for more than she was willing to offer. Wasn't a fling better than nothing? Maybe, with time, Mercedes would start wanting a deeper connection.

Syd twisted a branch away and steered her thoughts back on track. Right now, their future didn't matter. They had tonight and Syd intended to make it count. She didn't want to drive Mercedes away by putting her on the spot. Declaring love would only invite rejection; Mercedes's comments had just made that perfectly clear. Suppressing the emotions that nearly choked her, Syd found Mercedes's lips and used her tongue to part them, delving into the moist warmth of her mouth. With a tug, she lowered Mercedes against their sacred oak tree. Here, she would seal her old memories with new ones. Sooner or later, both would fade.

She almost shook her head as the lie rolled through her

mind. The old memories hadn't faded in the least. They'd just become more bearable with time. She moved between Mercedes's parted thighs and kissed her with everything she had, hoping Mercedes felt the depth of her passion. With her very being, she needed Mercedes to take a memory of their lovemaking away with her, something that would niggle at her mind on lonely nights and, God forbid, when she was in the arms of another woman. Maybe, just maybe, Mercedes would heed the message of her heart and find a way back.

Syd pushed all negative thoughts aside. There was too little time to be consumed by the hurt. She'd have more than enough time to deal with that when Mercedes left her once again. Mercedes cupped her face and pulled her closer, running her hands through Syd's hair, then down her back, over the contours of her denim-clad ass. Syd thrust against her, wanting to be inside her, to feel her jerk and spasm with the release of an orgasm. Jesus, she wanted this woman right now, tomorrow, and forever. It didn't matter whether Mercedes wanted the same thing.

Feeling Mercedes buck against her, Syd reached down and opened the clasp of her jeans. Mercedes wove her hands between them as well and frantically worked the button fly of Syd's jeans, then pushed her fingers past her briefs. Wiggling further, she thrust inside.

Syd groaned, arched toward her, and breathlessly panted, "Deeper."

Mercedes obliged by drilling deeper. "God, I've wanted to do that all fucking evening."

Syd rode her fingers and pumped her hips, reaching for climax. Chips of moonlight speckled Mercedes's eyes and highlighted her expression. Syd almost gasped at the compassion she saw there. It was written all over her lovely face. How fitting she'd catch a glimpse of it here, beneath the spot where their love had been born, where her heart had been given to Mercedes, where her heart still remained. Her body ached to the core for release, but with the pressure came an overwhelming urge to tell Mercedes that she loved her, that she always had and knew she always would. Yet something in Mercedes's expression had already changed and her stare became distant, forcing Syd to hold her tongue. What was the point of releasing her secret if those words would be lost on deaf ears, or on a closed heart?

She reached down and stilled Mercedes's hand, halting those wild thrusts. "Here, it's together only."

Mercedes quivered and then a smile spread across her lips. She slowly nodded and with shaking hands and laughter, they tore at each other's clothing, kissing wet paths across one another, clinging, grasping, kissing.

Mercedes wrapped her legs around Syd's waist and pulled her down. "Make love to me, Syd."

The plea was a whisper against her ear. Syd's stomach stirred as her heart fluttered out of control. She closed her eyes and sensually dragged her tongue from corner to corner across Mercedes's lips before snaking into her mouth. Mercedes released a sexy sigh and tightened her grip around Syd's neck. Tight with need, flesh against flesh, Syd pumped, her mind and body finally attuned to a single purpose. She knew what Mercedes wanted and she would give it to her.

Blocking everything else from her mind, Syd wedged her hand between then, found Mercedes's wet opening, and pressed her fingers inside. Mercedes whipped her head back and released that sweet cry Syd knew would forever be embedded in her mind. And then they were both falling over the brink, into oblivion…into nothing. And even as she floated in bliss, Syd couldn't ignore the words that rang insistently in her head.

Leaning into Mercedes, she whispered against her cheek, "I love you. Please don't go."

❖

Mercedes awoke with an easy smile. Her insides ached with sweet pain and her lips felt blissfully swollen from so much kissing. She moaned and stretched out across Syd's bed only to find the other half empty. She fingered the lone pillow, certain she remembered Syd cursing when the phone rang a few hours after they walked back here. Something about a birth, and damn animals, and a few other things that were hazy at the moment.

I love you.

Had that been a dream or had Syd declared her love last night under the oak tree? Mercedes was certain she hadn't dreamed it. She could almost physically remember the drop of her heart and then the sudden rise of adrenaline to have heard the words.

Syd loved her.

Good Lord, how did she feel about that? Good? Great? Sad?

She felt…in love. And she needed to say those words to Syd, right this very minute. Without hesitation, she dived for the phone by the bed and dialed Syd's cell, only to hear a ring tone sound in the living room.

"Damn it!" She shook her head in disbelief and glanced at the clock. Only a few more hours before that bird carried her back to LA…back to the real world. Surely Syd would return to see her off.

Mercedes mentally rehearsed what she would say. First, she would tell the truth—that she loved Syd, that the feelings she'd had as a kid had bloomed into something much deeper and she was old enough now to understand her emotions. Then she would ask Syd to share a piece of her life with her…maybe weekends at first, or a holiday, whatever they could spare. Maybe after getting used to LA, Syd might consider giving up this ranch life. She was a strong woman and she could find work anywhere…in LA.

Would Syd be willing to give up this ranching dream of hers so they could be together? Mercedes prayed she would. Eventually.

❖

Syd resisted the urge to glance at her watch as time crawled by. Her thoughts were never too far from Mercedes, hadn't been throughout the whole night. Their last night together before Mercedes flew out of her life again, and she wasn't there to hold her, to fuck her, or imprint unforgettable images upon her heart.

This time of year, no one got much sleep at the D&M Cattle Company. The horses were in foal and the cows were still calving every day. Syd sighed, overcome with fatigue. Now that she was standing in for Miller, the calls for help came to her and she'd answered two since she and Mercedes had returned to the ranch house.

Syd ran her hands through her hair and down over her face. Nearly done, she couldn't wait to get back to Mercedes. Her luck had held and the cow that had struggled for the past few hours had finally delivered her calf and placenta right on cue. Syd gave the new mother one last check, then returned to the pickup and tossed her bag in the bed of the truck. The sky was light pink with morning rays. Fuck, it was late. Too late.

There was no way she could make it back to the ranch before Mercedes had to leave for the airport, before she walked out of Syd's life for good.

Syd's hands shook on the steering wheel. She was in love—breathless, eating through her soul, out of her mind love. It was terrifying as much as it was numbing…and emotional. She wanted to fall to her knees and cry, to scream, to beat her hands against the dirt ground…then fall over in a heap and wallow in misery. What in the hell was she supposed to do? Mercedes had made it plain she didn't want to extend their "dates" past this weekend. Syd didn't need a more categorical rejection. Mercedes didn't even react when Syd told her she loved her last night. Syd knew she wasn't sleeping at the time. She'd felt a slight reaction, a stiffening of her shoulders. The wordless response still hurt.

Syd's heart cramped in her chest at the thought that there couldn't be anything further, and now it looked like she would not even get to say good-bye, to see that face one last time… or hear Mercedes scream as she came one more time. Syd couldn't do it. She couldn't let Mercedes leave without telling her again, "Please don't leave me—don't go. I love you."

Hearing the words spoken out loud gave her confidence that she was making the right decision. She scrabbled in the truck for her cell phone, shoving tools and ropes aside in a panic. Then she remembered being only half awake and leaving it on the couch where she'd gotten dressed. A knot tightened in her gut, threatening to choke the life from her body.

She'd left her only means of communication at home— with Mercedes.

❖

"Where the fuck is she?" Mercedes paced in the driveway, already fifteen minutes late in leaving. She still had to return the rental and check in. If she didn't hurry, she'd never make her flight on time.

Was that such a bad thing? Couldn't she take a later flight? Maybe a day later? She stared around, hoping Syd had just lost track of time while she tended the animals. Her head throbbed with tension and she kicked at the pebbles, sickness coiling in her stomach like an icy snake. How bad she'd wanted to tell Syd good-bye face-to-face this time, and not in a stinking letter that sounded more pathetic every time she thought about the words she'd written so many years ago.

What a freak she was to have thought there could ever be anything more. The woman lived and breathed this ranch, and Mercedes was a fool to think she'd give up any part of it for her. Hell, she couldn't even prioritize Mercedes enough to spare a good-bye now, after saying she loved her. The words rang false, spoiled by Syd's actions.

Mercedes continued her pacing, desperate to hear the roar of her truck speeding down the driveway. After several agonizing minutes, she realized Syd was playing the same shitty game she'd played so many years ago. She'd gotten what she wanted and now she had more important things to do. The ranch came first. Period.

With a clenching of her jaw, Mercedes decided today was her lucky day…she could make a graceful exit and avoid the humiliation of chasing Syd. Chasing wasn't her style anyway. She would phone Syd in a few days' time, a friendly no-strings call. If she was going to visit the ranch on occasion, at least they could be on civil terms. She couldn't imagine settling for a casual friendship with Syd, and nothing more. Besides, casual friends knew how to keep their hands off each other.

With a despondent sigh, Mercedes climbed into the car and revved the engine to life. Feeling heartstrings roping around her, she took one last glance at the ranch and punched the gas. Sydney Campbell could go to hell for all she cared.

By the time she'd returned the rental and boarded her flight, her mood had turned lethal. She fell into the window seat and fumed, not only at Syd but at herself. What had she done to let Syd know she wanted more, to invite Syd to put her first this morning? Nothing. Absolutely nothing. In fact, she'd all but told Syd there couldn't be more. Why hadn't Syd seen the lie written all over her face? Couldn't she feel it?

Mercedes stared out the window as the plane rolled toward the runway, her mind reeling, her heart stammering, and her love…being left behind. She let herself indulge once again in a last hopeless fantasy that Syd would show up, stop her, toss her over her shoulder and carry her off this plane just like in the movies. But the flight attendants secured the hatches and waved the safety instructions sheet. People said good-bye to loved ones and put their cell phones away.

Mercedes took a final look at hers, just in case there was a message, then turned it off. As the plane lifted into the air, she watched the ground recede until all she could see was puffy clouds, then she let loose her tears in a blinding stream.

Chapter Sixteen

The Edwards case was giving Mercedes migraines, measuring blood splatter, redoing the formulas and equations, making sure no stone had been left unturned. The son of a bitch had already gotten off once due to poor DNA samples; she'd be damned if he got off this time. She would see that serial killer behind bars if it was the last thing she did. The world would never know how unsafe they were with him on the streets, on the hunt for more female blood.

Mercedes didn't know when a case had stressed her so much. Worse, every time she talked to her daddy, she found herself crying, and homesick. She wasn't surprised when he announced his retirement. He was making Syd an equal partner. Mercedes knew she should have expected that too, but it landed like a blow, crushing the fantasies she'd been clinging to—that she would go see Syd once the Edwards trial was over and ask her to come to LA to visit, then Syd would decide to stay…

Almost a month had passed since the wedding and they hadn't spoken. A thousand times Mercedes had picked up the phone, but she kept thinking about the last time she'd waited for Syd to call. Years had passed and Syd hadn't cared enough to pick up the phone. Was it any different now? Mercedes wanted to find out, so she was waiting for Syd to make the first move.

Her daddy's news explained why she hadn't. Syd deserved the partnership; she'd earned the privilege with her hard work and dedication. And her daddy had a right to retire. He and Nelda planned to purchase a quaint little vacation home on the Florida Keys where the two snowbirds could escape from the bitter Colorado cold during the winter months. He'd e-mailed pictures of the cute little condo surrounded by fruit trees and well-kept green grass. Mercedes envisioned him smiling brightly while he cruised the golf courses or went out fishing. She ached to be close to him, close to all of them.

Damn if she didn't miss that stupid ranch, and the air. As soon as she'd landed in LA, the smog had invaded her lungs like a heavy gray blanket. Could she seriously miss…home, when she'd fought so hard to stay so far away from the ranch? Yet here she was, wishing for things half a map away, moping for Syd.

Of course, Darlene had called, she'd left several messages, but Mercedes couldn't bring herself to speak to her. Just hearing her happy reports about love and the future she planned with Seth was torture. Mercedes wasn't ready to have conversations about another bridesmaid dress for someone else's dream wedding. She was back in the swing of things, leaving behind romance, long-distance relationships, and heaven forbid, love. Her life was perfect, even if Sydney Campbell wanted no part in it. And maybe it was for the best. Love…was dangerous. It had the power to cloud one's judgment and confuse rational thought.

Syd knew better than to throw away the life she loved, and Mercedes realized she loved Syd for who she was. It was wrong to hope she would leave the ranch and turn into someone else. All Syd could ever be in LA was a transplant pining for the wide-open spaces. With a grunt, Mercedes leaned back in her desk chair. She'd never ask her to leave her dreams behind. That wasn't love, it was selfishness. There was only one way she and Syd would have a future, if Syd even wanted one— Mercedes would have to go back home.

She shook her head at the thought and concentrated on the documents in front of her. That wasn't going to happen. How would it ever work? She had a career, and while her work disillusioned her, she couldn't see herself trading it for an apron and the kitchen sink as a rancher's wife. Mercedes tapped her pen against the side of her desk, her mind busily offering alternatives.

There were people in her field who worked from home as expert witnesses and consultants. With all the staffing cutbacks, some departments preferred to hire independents. Was that something she could consider?

❖

Sydney backed the horse out of the stall and reached for a brush. Lovesick, that's what she was. And miserable. God, she couldn't think straight, and she was doing a piss-ass job running the ranch that might soon be half hers. She'd been awestruck when Miller returned and offered her an equal partnership, telling her it was time for him to step aside and enjoy his retirement.

Syd had swallowed back tears—not only from his offer, but because looking into his eyes was like looking into the future. If she took his offer, it would seal her fate. She would never leave Larimer County. She would be choosing this life knowing she would never share it with Mercedes. Syd ached, she missed her so badly…her smile, her laugh, her parted lips.

Growling, she stroked the brush against the colt's flank and sent dust flying from his coat. She wished she could sweep the images of Mercedes from her mind with the same ease.

Darlene refilled the horses' feed and leaned against the stall door. "So, how long are you going to mope around here like you've lost your best friend?"

"I told you, I'm not talking about this with you anymore."

"We didn't talk about it the last time, or the time before that, or the time before that." When Syd looked over at her, Darlene shrugged. "Sorry, I'm a persistent little thing."

"Where's that hunk of yours?" Syd absently stroked the colt's face and blew up his nose. She received a friendly snort in return.

"No, no, no. You are *not* changing the subject on me. This is about you and Mercedes, not my sexy-ass cowboy."

Syd ignored her and continued grooming on the far side.

"Hello? I'm talking to you."

"No, you're not. You're talking to yourself."

Darlene moved away from the stable door and flipped an empty feed bucket upside down, then perched on it, only feet away from Syd. "I need to talk to you about something."

"Does it have to do with Mercedes?"

"Yes."

Syd shook her head. "Then I don't want to hear it, and that's final. Please leave it alone, okay?"

"I took the note," Darlene said.

"What note?" Syd popped the colt's rear end and he scurried into his stall. She followed him and slid the bar into place.

"The one Mercedes left for you…when she went to college."

Syd turned her head sharply. "What are you talking about?"

"She left you a good-bye note asking you to call her." Darlene held her head high. If there was any shame in what she was admitting, it didn't show in her expression.

"You read it?" Syd frowned. "Why didn't you say something...why did you take it?"

"Because she was spoiled, and everything revolved around her. She didn't love you. You were way too good for her. Hell, you've always been too good for her."

Syd wasn't sure if she should be angry. Darlene was telling her that her life could have turned out differently, that Mercedes hadn't just moved on without a thought.

"I let her go," Syd said. "I thought that was what she wanted."

"You would have been kicked to the curb if you hadn't," Darlene said. "Maybe she would have played with you for a while longer, but she was too headstrong, with nothing but her career in her sights. She would have clawed her way to the top right over your shredded heart."

"That should have been my choice to make, not yours."

Darlene nodded. "That's true. But I adore you, and I couldn't stand to think of her dragging you along for her ride."

"Why tell me now...after all these years?"

"Because she loves you and I'm the only sister she's got. But that doesn't change the fact she's self-centered and arrogant, with that 'no one is above me' attitude. Admit it. She's a bitch." Darlene smiled.

Syd leaned against the wall for support. Mercedes had wanted her after all. Adrenaline pumped through her veins borne on a rush of bittersweet memories. Had Darlene robbed her of love? Looking down over Darlene now, her shoulders squared, her face defiant, Syd knew she hadn't. Any life she could have had with Mercedes all those years ago would have been lost in the whirlwind of college and career. Syd was sure of that. It would have ended horribly, with Syd probably tucking her tail between her legs and crawling back home.

"You're right, it wouldn't have worked."

"I know." Darlene stood and pushed the bucket away with her booted foot. "But it can now. She's changed, and you did that. Her trip back here, seeing you, it changed her and I know in my heart she's ready now. Go get her."

Syd laughed. "She's not a steer, Darlene. I can't just rope her and expect her to lie still while I slap my brand on her rump."

"I don't know about that." Darlene grinned. "Sure looked to me like you already did that."

With a groan, Syd said, "I can't fit inside her world and I know better than to try. Don't you understand that?"

"Understand what?" Miller strolled into the barn.

"Nothing," Syd began. "We were just saying—"

"That Syd needs to go get that dang foul-mouthed sister of mine and bring her home," Darlene interjeced with a self-satisfied smirk.

Miller nodded. "I agree. It's time for you to stop moping around this damn ranch and go drag her ass back where she belongs."

Syd stood in shocked silence. She and Miller had never talked about Mercedes aside from what he shared about her life in LA. How had he guessed so much?

He took a deliberate step toward her and thrust a folded envelope into her grasp. "She's as miserable as you are, and though she won't admit it, she wants to be here. It's your job to take care of this ranch. You can start by going to get my baby and bringing her home."

Syd unfolded the paperwork and bit back a gasp when she found two plane tickets, one round trip, the other one way. Destination: Los Angeles.

She met his gaze, but was lost for words.

"Don't be a fool, Sydney." He turned and left the barn.

❖

Mercedes fought back her tears as she wove through the combustion of LA traffic. The Edwards trial was a total bust. All that hard work, all those long hours proving his guilt, had counted for nothing. The bastard was guilty, and she'd proven that during her grueling hours on the stand. She'd overturned every argument from his defense team and made the expert witnesses they'd called to refute her look like complete idiots. Hell, she'd gone as far as to make their contentions seem laughable, leaving no room for doubt in the jury's minds.

And for what? She'd wasted precious time slaving over this case when she could have taken a few extra days at the ranch. Now all her work had been undone by an alibi witness who came forward at the last minute. The defense had argued evidence contamination all the way through the trial, and finally, with the new witness, the jury had opted for caution. This was a death penalty case. They didn't want to convict the wrong man, so Edwards had walked.

Fuck! What the hell was she doing here, in this town, with crime at its highest and every damn case a lottery? She was selling her soul for a lousy paycheck, for that perfect condo, for her so-called perfect life. What a fucking joke that was. Her life was so far from the perfect glossy magazine images she'd imagined all those years ago. The smog had supposedly improved, but some days it still hovered over the landscape like a toxin cloud. God, how she missed the fresh air on the ranch. She even missed the damn crickets and frogs singing long into the night.

A car in front of her slammed on its brakes. Mercedes cursed, and with the experience gained only from living in such a congested city, she glanced in her side mirror and slid smartly into the other lane like a professional driver. She barely missed the tail end of a sedan driven by a middle-aged creep who was too busy sightseeing to pay attention to the traffic around him.

She bellowed "Asshole!" through the convertible top, then darted past him.

When she merged back into the slow lane, she took a deep breath and tried to calm her frazzled nerves. She felt lost and depressed, but the feeling wasn't new. It wasn't brought on by having to watch a serial killer walk out of the courtroom scot-free. That made her angry and cynical, like every other professional involved in the case. But there was something else gnawing at her.

An image of Syd fluttered through her mind as she took an off-ramp into a higher priced area of the city. She wondered what Syd was doing right now, with the ranch an hour ahead of LA. Probably training one of the young quarter horses, her posture straight and her head held high, those delicious legs wrapped around the beast. Mercedes's pussy pulsed with the image. God, she missed her, wished she was sitting on the split-rail back on the ranch, watching her from afar. Did Syd miss her, too? Had she thought about her? Did she yearn the way Mercedes did, aching for her touch?

Slowing down, she wove around some teenagers playing football in the street. She was anxious to get home and swap her binding business suit for a comfortable pair of pajamas. A thought slipped into her mind. Living in this city, surrounded by concrete and cars, the kids she'd passed would never know what it was like to climb trees to look out over the mountains. They'd never swing from a rope to drop into a pond, or sleep under the stars.

"I wanna go home." The statement was out of her mouth before she ever knew it rested in her mind. She blinked hard, unable to believe she'd spoken the words aloud. A smile stretched the width of her heart. Home... Home was in Colorado, on that damn ranch, with all those stinky horses and cattle, with her family.

Mercedes reached for the remote control and opened the security barrier, her mind filled with plans. She knew people she could talk to about working freelance. She could split her time, basing herself at the ranch and traveling when she had a case to work. Maybe she could offer consultancy services to writers and researchers. She drove the car into her reserved parking bay, closed the top, and almost ran up the steps to the courtyard.

She stopped cold in her tracks when her gaze fell upon a familiar figure below her porch. Syd was slowly pacing, her thighs encased in loose denim, her body strong inside a red-checked shirt. She looked uneasy and out of place, the gray stucco condo completely wrong as her backdrop. Only mountains and acres of land should dare surround her.

A sob escaped Mercedes and before she could take another step, Syd was there, holding her, lovingly caressing her face, cupping her cheeks. Tilting Mercedes's head up and looking into her eyes, Syd took a shaky breath. Her dark, penetrating eyes looked right into Mercedes's soul as she said, "I love you."

With a feather-light touch of lips, Mercedes knew she was

going home—not home to a place, but home to a heart. "I love you, too, Syd," she said. "I have for thirteen years."

Syd thumbed a path across Mercedes's bottom lip. "I know, and I want the next thirteen years with you so we can prove it."

About the Author

Larkin Rose lives in a "blink and you've missed it" town in the beautiful state of South Carolina with her partner, Rose (hence the pen name), a portion of their seven brats, a chunky grandson, and too many animals to name. Her writing career began two years ago when the voices in her head wouldn't stop their constant chatter. After ruling out multiple personalities, and hitting the keyboard, a writer was born.

Books Available From Bold Strokes Books

No Leavin' Love by Larkin Rose. Beautiful, successful Mercedes Miller thinks she can resume her affair with ranch foreman Sydney Campbell, but the rules have changed. (978-1-60282-079-1)

Between the Lines by Bobbi Marolt. When romance writer Gail Prescott meets actress Tannen Albright, she develops feelings that she usually only experiences through her characters. (978-1-60282-078-4)

Blue Skies by Ali Vali. Commander Berkley Levine leads an elite group of pilots on missions ordered by her ex-lover Captain Aidan Sullivan and everything is on the line—including love. (978-1-60282-077-7)

The Lure by Felice Picano. When Noel Cummings is recruited by the police to go undercover to find a killer, his life will never be the same. (978-1-60282-076-0)

Death of a Dying Man by J.M. Redmann. Mickey Knight, Private Eye and partner of Dr. Cordelia James, doesn't need a drop-dead gorgeous assistant—not until nature steps in. (978-1-60282-075-3)

Justice for All by Radclyffe. Dell Mitchell goes undercover to expose a human traffic ring and ends up in the middle of an even deadlier conspiracy. (978-1-60282-074-6)

Sanctuary by I. Beacham. Cate Canton faces one major obstacle to her goal of crushing her business rival, Dita Newton—her uncontrollable attraction to Dita. (978-1-60282-055-5)

The Sublime and Spirited Voyage of Original Sin by Colette Moody. Pirate Gayle Malvern finds the presence of an abducted seamstress, Celia Pierce, a welcome distraction until the captive comes to mean more to her than is wise. (978-1-60282-054-8)

Suspect Passions by VK Powell. Can two women, a city attorney and a beat cop, put aside their differences long enough to see that they're perfect for each other? (978-1-60282-053-1)

Just Business by Julie Cannon. Two women who come together—each for her own selfish needs—discover that love can never be as simple as a business transaction. (978-1-60282-052-4)

Sistine Heresy by Justine Saracen. Adrianna Borgia, survivor of the Borgia court, presents Michelangelo with the greatest temptations of his life while struggling with soul-threatening desires for the painter Raphaela. (978-1-60282-051-7)

Radical Encounters by Radclyffe. An out-of-bounds, outside-the-lines collection of provocative, superheated erotica by award-winning romance and erotica author Radclyffe. (978-1-60282-050-0)

Thief of Always by Kim Baldwin & Xenia Alexiou. Stealing a diamond to save the world should be easy for Elite Operative Mishael Taylor, but she didn't figure on love getting in the way. (978-1-60282-049-4)

X by JD Glass. When X-hacker Charlie Riven is framed for a crime she didn't commit, she accepts help from an unlikely source—sexy Treasury Agent Elaine Harper. (978-1-60282-048-7)

The Middle of Somewhere by Clifford Henderson. Eadie T. Pratt sets out on a road trip in search of a new life and ends up in the middle of somewhere she never expected. (978-1-60282-047-0)

Paybacks by Gabrielle Goldsby. Cameron Howard wants to avoid her old nemesis Mackenzie Brandt but their high school reunion brings up more than just memories. (978-1-60282-046-3)

Uncross My Heart by Andrews & Austin. When a radio talk show diva sets out to interview a female priest, the two women end up at odds and neither heaven nor earth is safe from their feelings. (978-1-60282-045-6)

Fireside by Cate Culpepper. Mac, a therapist, and Abby, a nurse, fall in love against the backdrop of friendship, healing, and defending one's own within the Fireside shelter. (978-1-60282-044-9)

A Pirate's Heart by Catherine Friend. When rare book librarian Emma Boyd searches for a long-lost treasure map, she learns the hard way that pirates still exist in today's world—some modern pirates steal maps, others steal hearts. (978-1-60282-040-1)

Trails Merge by Rachel Spangler. Parker Riley escapes the high-powered world of politics to Campbell Carson's ski resort—and their mutual attraction produces anything but smooth running. (978-1-60282-039-5)

Dreams of Bali by C.J. Harte. Madison Barnes worships work, power, and success, and she's never allowed anyone to interfere—that is, until she runs into Karlie Henderson Stockard. Aeros EBook (978-1-60282-070-8)

The Limits of Justice by John Morgan Wilson. Benjamin Justice and reporter Alexandra Templeton search for a killer in a mysterious compound in the remote California desert. (978-1-60282-060-9)

Designed for Love by Erin Dutton. Jillian Sealy and Wil Johnson don't much like each other, but they do have to work together—and what they desire most is not what either of them had planned. (978-1-60282-038-8)

Calling the Dead by Ali Vali. Six months after Hurricane Katrina, NOLA Detective Sept Savoie is a cop who thinks making a relationship work is harder than catching a serial killer—but her current case may prove her wrong. (978-1-60282-037-1)

Shots Fired by MJ Williamz. Kyla and Echo seem to have the perfect relationship and the perfect life until someone shoots at Kyla—and Echo is the most likely suspect. (978-1-60282-035-7)

truelesbianlove.com by Carsen Taite. Mackenzie Lewis and Dr. Jordan Wagner have very different ideas about love, but they discover that truelesbianlove is closer than a click away. Aeros EBook (978-1-60282-069-2)

Justice at Risk by John Morgan Wilson. Benjamin Justice's blind date leads to a rare opportunity for legitimate work, but a reckless risk changes his life forever. (978-1-60282-059-3)

Run to Me by Lisa Girolami. Burned by the four-letter word called love, the only thing Beth Standish wants to do is run for—or maybe from—her life. (978-1-60282-034-0)